MAID OF SHERWOOD

SHANTI KRISHNAMURTY

License Notes

Cover design by Damon of damonza.com
Formatting by RikHall.com

Acknowledgements

First, I'd like to acknowledge my fabulous cover artist, Damon of damonza.com, for all his hard work. His cover reflects my vision exactly.

To Jenni, who continues to be an inspiration with every word challenge; Denise, who pokes and prods at me until I write…and then pokes at me some more. And for my sister, Rama, who tells me over and over and over that I have the talent and not to listen to my inner demons.

Without them, and numerous others, I wouldn't have gone forward with my dreams. There are no words for what they have brought to my life.

Dedication

For God, who led me every step of the way; my amazing husband, without whom this dream would mean less than nothing, and to G.B. Krishnamurty, the best Daddy a girl could ever wish for.

Chapter One:

"Did you know Nottingham Castle has ghosts you can see?" When Marian shook her head, Will continued. "They look like little boys and play tricks on everyone they do not like."

"How can you be sure they actually exist?" To Marian's knowledge, Will Scarlett had never been beyond Sherwood Forest, let alone to the castle. She pushed her way through the overgrown English oaks and into a small clearing. The tall green grass had been trampled flat, as though by horses' hooves. Her hand involuntarily dropped to the scabbard at her waist. Rumor had it the sheriff's men refused to enter the woods surrounding Nottingham Castle; the woods were thick and lush even during the harshest winters but she was not willing to take a chance. Men travelling through Sherwood had vanished without a trace and Marian was not sure only outlaws were at fault.

Will followed her, one hand resting on the pommel of his sword. "Of course the ghosts exist. James travelled to the castle nearly two weeks ago and heard them screaming on the battlements."

"It is nonsense," Marian declared. She took her hand off the worn leather scabbard and pushed a stray curl of hair behind her ear. "Next you will be telling me you believe in the fairies, too." She turned to face him.

"Something is odd about this forest, Marian. You cannot deny it, and fairies make sense. What else could keep the forest so green all year around?"

She crinkled her nose at him. "I will believe in fairies when I see the ghosts for myself."

The tall seventeen year old laughed. "The day your mother allows you near Nottingham Castle…"

"Is the day you will join Hood's band of Merry Men!" Marian finished. It was an old joke between them. Beatrix du Luc, with bloodlines dating all the way back to Queen Guinevere and King Arthur; loyal subject of King Richard, would never dream of allowing her daughter anywhere near a castle where Prince John held court. "Want to go in further?"

Will tugged at the wispy beard sprouting from his chin. "Aunt Constance has chores for me to finish."

"Well, I am going," Marian declared. "If I go home now, Mother will make me try on the May gown again, even though the seamstress is coming tomorrow."

"Does she still want to find you a husband?"

"It is all she ever talks about." Marian raised her voice in a fair imitation of Mother's. "'Marian, dear, if you wear nothing but breeches, you shall never find a husband worthy of your bloodlines.'" Her voice dropped. "What she cannot understand is that I do not want the husband she chooses." She thought of her bedecked and bejeweled mother and grimaced. "All *she* cares about is what ribbons best match her eyes. I can only imagine the man she would choose for me."

"At least she loves you," Will said forlornly. "It could be worse. You could not have a mother."

Marian placed on hand on her friend's shoulder. "I am sorry, Will. I wish there was something I could do."

"Until there is proof the sheriff killed her, no-one can do anything. I hope someone, somewhere, gives that fatherless son of a goat everything he deserves."

A gruff voice spoke from the tree line. "Want to 'elp with that?"

Marian and Will whirled, swords pulling free from their respective sheaths as they scanned the empty clearing.

An enormous man pushed his way past branches hanging heavy with green-brown moss. His arms were corded with muscle and he held a large quarterstaff in one giant hand.

"Who are you?" Will demanded, pushing Marian behind him.

Marian yelped, shoved his arm down, and stepped forward to stand at his side.

2

Planting the quarterstaff in the dirt, the stranger leaned on it. The wood creaked under his weight. "Name is Little John."

Will shrugged. "Means nothing to me," he said.

"How do we know you are not one of the sheriff's men?" Marian questioned.

Little John's laughter rumbled low in his chest. "I would not be wearin' this if I worked with the sheriff." He motioned to his clothing; carefully cobbled scraps of mottled green and brown leather.

"It could still be a trick," Marian said suspiciously.

The other man shrugged. "Either y' believe me, or y' do not."

Will sheathed his sword. "I believe him."

"Well, then, that brings me back to the first question. Do you want to 'elp us destroy the sheriff?" Little John leaned harder on his quarterstaff and the wood groaned louder.

Sheathing her sword, Marian nodded. "When do we start?"

"Not you. Only him." Little John gestured towards Will with his chin. "Though yer good with a sword. Come back 'ere after the Fest'val. As near t' sundown as you can get."

"I will be here," Will shook the hand Little John held out.

"Alone," the big man tossed the instruction back over his shoulder before vanishing back into the overgrowth.

"What was that about?" Marian asked. "And why am I forbidden? Everyone in town would benefit from the destruction of the sheriff, not just you."

Will stepped away from her before he answered, the glint in his eyes telling Marian she would not like what he said. "Maybe it is because you're a girl."

"I am a better swordsman than you, Will Scarlett!" Marian retorted.

"Do you not mean swords*woman*?" Her friend said, staying out of her reach.

"Go away, Will. Go do your chores." Marian waved him off.

Will sobered. "Be careful, Marian. Sherwood is not safe."

"Now you sound like my mother," she grumbled. "I have my sword," she patted the butter soft leather scabbard. "I can take care of myself."

3

"I know you can," her friend said. "But your mother would never forgive either of us if something happened to you."

"Mother's forgiveness is not high on my list of priorities. I think we started arguing the day I opened my eyes and saw her face."

"Even so…" Concerned brown eyes caught her cornflower blue gaze. "I would not want to see her truly angry."

"I will be careful, if that will get you to leave. I just—want to be alone before I have to go back." Marian watched as he slipped through the trees, leaves barely rustling in his wake. In his absence, the not quite silence she loved re-exerted itself. The shrill 'cheep-cheep' of hungry newborn birds could be heard over quiet rustling in the forest deadfall. Unbuckling the strap which held her scabbard around her waist, she carefully laid it on the grass before seating herself next to it. Truthfully, she had no desire to go deeper into the forest. Closing her eyes, she sighed. Little John was obviously an outlaw, but he was just as obviously not a threat to her, nor to anyone else not associated with the sheriff. She let her mind drift. What if Little John could overthrow the sheriff and, ultimately, Prince John's iron rule? What would that mean for England?

Thud!

Marian's eyes shot open and she stared at the arrow buried in the dirt next to her sword. Even as she leapt to her feet, her fingers fumbling the sword from its sheath, a tall man swung down from the limb of a misshapen oak to land in front of her.

"Who are you?" His voice sent shivers down her spine. "What are you doing in my forest?"

Her eyebrows crawled into her hairline. "*Your* forest? I believe Sherwood belongs to the king, as does all of England."

Eyes the color of a foggy morning captured and held her in their depths. His face, with its sharply defined cheekbones and full, almost pouting, lips, was dappled by the fading sunlight. "I hold these forests for King Richard." The stranger's fingers hovered at his shoulder, where she could see the tip of the longbow strapped across his back. "What is your excuse for being here?"

Marian's jaw clenched. No matter how handsome he was, he had no call to speak to her so demandingly. "And does King Richard approve of you accosting every girl you come across?"

He winked at her. "Only pretty ones holding swords."

"I—I come here to escape my fate." She flushed. What a stupid thing to say!

"How curious," the man said. "I live here for the same reason." Reaching behind him, he lifted the longbow off his back and set it on the grass next to her empty sheath. "Now, if you do not plan on killing me, would you do me the courtesy of sheathing your blade?"

"I have no idea who you are," Marian said. "Why should I trust you?"

"I did not kill you when I could have." He smiled. Marian's heart leapt.

"Tell me your name," she demanded. When he cocked an eyebrow at her, she continued. "Call it an act of good faith."

"Very well. I am Robin." He spread his empty arms, palm up. "As you can clearly see, I am no threat to you."

Marian was not sure he was right. The man's physical presence was enough to make her breath catch in her throat, though she tried hard to conceal it. She cautiously stepped closer to him, bent down and picked up her sheath. As she slid the sword home, she glanced at him through lowered lashes. Hair the color of an autumn sunset was tied back away from his face, but a few reddish gold pieces had escaped their noose and hung, brushing against his broad shoulders. It would be nothing, Marian thought, to loosen the leather strap and allow her fingers to run wild through the strands of his hair, combing it back as she leaned forward and...

"Are you going to stare at me all night?" Robin's voice cut through her daydream and she jerked upright, the sheathed sword dangling loosely from her grip.

"What? No. I mean...I was not..." She blushed.

He grinned at her consternation. "You were, but since *I* am a gentleman, I will not mention it again." Robin lowered his arms. "Shall we sit?" He followed his own advice.

5

Sitting with, and speaking to, a strange man was something Mother would never condone. Marian sat down immediately.

"Now, then, since I have been kind enough to share my name with you, would you do me the kindness of returning the favor?"

"You are very well spoken for a—a..."

"The word you are searching for is 'outlaw,'" Robin said.

Marian's eyes widened. "You are an outlaw? Have you heard of Hood? Are you part of his band?"

"Is he not the outlaw king, or some such rubbish?" Robin leaned back on his hands and stretched his legs out. He wore the same cobbled materials Little John had sported.

Marian could not help it. She leapt to Hood's defense. "He steals monies from the wealthy, and gives it to the poor so they can eat. I hardly think that is rubbish!"

Robin nodded. "I see. You're one of those poor town girls who thinks he does no wrong and secretly wants to be betrothed to him."

"I most certainly do *not*!" Marian protested, but the red creeping up her face turned her protest into truth.

"You do!" He laughed and she barely resisted the urge to slap him.

"Whether I do or not is none of your concern, since you are not him, nor one of his Merry Men."

"What if I was?"

"What if you were what? One of Hood's men?"

Robin shook his head. "What if I was Hood himself? Would you feel the same way?"

Marian's breath caught at the idea. "I hardly know you," she protested.

"You do not know *him* at all. Only stories of him." Robin leaned close to her. "What makes him so different?"

"He actually stands up for us; stands up for everyone the prince and sheriff overtax, injure and murder. Hood stands for King Richard's beliefs while the king is away. He keeps us safe."

"You make him sound as near to sainthood as mortal man can come."

"He steals—"

"From the rich and gives to the poor," Robin finished. "Yes, you said that."

Marian leaned forward, her face inches from Robin's. "Why are you so determined to dismiss his accomplishments?"

Robin shrugged. "I am not. But he is only a man, trying to do what is right."

"But that is precisely my point," Marian said. "Most are so frightened of the sheriff and Prince John they refuse to fight against their tyranny."

"What would you have them do? Gather their hoes and cabbages and launch a campaign worthy of the Crusades?"

"My father always tells me even a pebble can change the course of a river." Marian tugged at a piece of grass until it came loose in her hand.

"Your father is a very wise man," Robin said. "And his daughter adheres well to his teachings."

"I...thank you," Marian said.

Robin picked up his longbow and rose to his feet. "As much as I have enjoyed this interlude, I fear I have certain—duties—that demand my attention. But before I go, am I allowed to know your name? Or is it a secret?"

"M—Marian," she stuttered. "My name is Marian."

He smiled at her one last time, and his light gray eyes lingered in her memory long after he had left the clearing.

Chapter Two:

"You were in Sherwood again, were you not?" Mother frowned as she seated herself at the dining table.

"I finished all my chores," Marian said. "The afternoon was mine to do with as I wished."

"That agreement only held so long as you came home before dark." Mother stated. She turned to Father. "Alan, talk some sense into her."

Father shrugged. "Your mother is right, Mari. You violated the agreement."

"By scant minutes!" Marian protested. "The sun was barely down."

Mother passed the bread basket across the table to Marian. "I allowed you, *against my better judgment*, to learn swordplay. The only restriction I placed on you was that you respect my wishes. And now I learn you have violated them."

"So now you are going to ban me from the forest?"

"It is three days until the May Festival, and you *are* its queen. I think staying in town until after Festival is a reasonable request."

Marian's jaw clenched. "The word 'request' usually implies the possibility of saying 'no.'"

"Mari, enough." Father said. "You will do as your mother wishes. It is not unreasonable, and you still have one more fitting for the gown, do you not?"

Marian sighed. "Yes, I do."

Father ladled vegetable soup into his bowl. "Then it is settled. Bea, have you told Mari the news?"

"What news?" Marian asked, dipping her bread into her soup bowl.

"We received a summons while you were in Sherwood." Mother smoothed a few stray blond curls away from her face. "After Festival, we leave for Nottingham Castle."

Marian's eyes widened. "What? Why?"

"Because we are royalty and we do whatever our prince requires of us," Mother said sharply.

"But you never wanted me to go to the castle."

"Our duties have nothing to do with our desires, Marian. We will be at the castle within two weeks. The sheriff is coming to escort us through the forest."

Father's low baritone cut through their conversation. "The prince himself wishes to hear me sing. It is a very great honor, and one I cannot refuse."

"But," Marian protested, "I've never been to court."

"I am aware of that, Marian," Mother said. "In truth, there is very little that will be required of you. We are going simply to show Prince John that the du Lucs are loyal to the throne. I do not want what happened to the children to happen to you." Her voice shook slightly.

"They were hostages, Mother. We're part of the royal family."

"Never assume that keeps us safe." The harshness of Mother's voice startled Marian. "Those boys were royalty, too. That did not stop John from murdering every one of them."

"Beatrix." Father's voice was mild, but Mother stopped speaking. She smoothed her already smooth hair again and leaned back in her chair.

"Eat your soup, Marian." Mother's voice was back to its usual honeyed tone.

Marian narrowed her eyes thoughtfully. For a split moment, Mother seemed unyielding and almost frightening. But that could not be right. It was only Mother, after all.

"Tomorrow I will summon the seamstress for your final fitting, then we can go into town and shop for more fabrics. The few gowns you have are wholly unsuitable for Prince John's court." Mother said.

Marian drew in a breath to protest, but released it at a glance from Father. She nodded her agreement instead.

"Well, since we are going to Nottingham, I need to finish my ballad," Father said. "I am hoping the castle historian will be in attendance when I perform."

"I did not know Nottingham still had a historian." Mother said. "I know there was one when I was at Henry's court, but it could not be the same woman. She was ancient when I knew her."

Father shrugged. "According to what I have heard, she would rather live near the forest than in the castle itself. She is rumored to be rather eccentric."

"Why did you leave King Henry's court, Mother?" Marian dipped her bread back into her soup before eating it.

Mother glanced at Father before answering. "After Henry died, I had no desire to stay. I had grown tired of court and Richard allowed me to leave to pursue my own interests."

"And marrying me was one of those interests," Father interjected.

Mother blushed. "Stop it, Alan."

"How did you two meet, anyway?" Anytime she had asked the question before, Mother had always deflected the conversation toward something else, but Marian hoped this time would be different.

Father laughed. "When I first saw your mother, she was standing knee deep in a pud—"

"Alan, this is hardly the time," Mother interrupted. "Marian, rather than ask unimportant questions, maybe your focus should be more on the meal in front of you."

"Yes, Mother." What could Mother possibly have been doing when they met? It was obviously something she was not proud of, and absolutely did *not* want Marian discovering, which made the mystery of it all the more intriguing. She pushed her bowl aside, half empty.

"May I be excused? I promised Will I would meet him after supper."

Mother raised her left eyebrow. "Not in Sherwood, I assume?"

Marian shook her head. "No. I am meeting him at his aunt's."

"Be sure you both stay in town," Mother said. "It is not safe in the forest after dark."

Marian's thoughts roamed back to the man she'd met; Robin. No, in this case, Mother was right. The forest was not safe, though not for the reasons she was likely thinking of.

"We will not leave his aunt," Marian promised. She cleared her bowl off the table and carried it into the kitchen. Leaving it on the long wooden table, she hurried out the kitchen door before Mother could change her mind.

"So," Will leaned against the doorjamb of his aunt's home. "You met a man in the woods, too. Did he invite you to a secret meeting, or am I the only one the outlaws are interested in?"

Marian sighed. As much as she loved Will, sometimes she detested his sense of humor. "I met one of the outlaws, as I told you. He did not say anything about secret meetings or—or much of anything else."

"Did he tell you he was one of Hood's?" Will picked a piece of wood off the edge of the door.

"No, but he did not say he was not, either." She frowned. "Come to think of it, he did not actually *say* much of anything." Except for learning his name, she did not know much about him, other than the fact that he lived in the woods. The prospect of finding out more was suddenly more important than learning Mother's secrets. "When did Little John want you to come back?"

Will narrowed his eyes. "What are you planning?"

Marian smiled. "I think Little John deserves a little 'surprise' for startling us, do you agree?"

"You and I have been friends since birth, Marian," Will started. "And how many times have you gotten me into trouble with Aunt Constance?"

"More times than I can count," Marian admitted. "But this is *important*, Will. I cannot tell you why, but I just know it is. Please let me tag along. I will be as silent as a grave. Little John will not even know I am there. I promise I will not get caught."

Will lowered his head for a minute as he thought. Looking Marian in the eyes, he finally spoke. "Be sure you do not. Neither of us knows what that man wants. What *either* man wants," he amended.

Marian released the breath she had been holding. "Thank you, Will. You will not regret it."

"I am pretty sure I already do," her friend said ruefully.

Marian smiled. "It will be fine," she promised. "Little John wants the same thing we do; freedom from the sheriff and Prince John. I doubt he will be angry at my intrusion, even if he finds out."

"Is that why you came over?" Will asked. "To get me to let you tag along?"

"No, actually I came to tell you about Mother, but I got distracted," Marian said.

Will frowned. "What about your mother? What's she done now?"

"That is it," Marian said. "She has not *done* anything. But we received a summons to court this afternoon and she began acting differently afterward." In a few succinct sentences, she told him of the incident at the dining table. "She was terrifying, Will. For a split second, I was sure she was not my mother at all, but someone completely different."

"I do not know of a single person who was not mad when Prince John hanged all those children. I am sure your mother's reaction was normal. I think your imagination is getting in the way of reality."

"You do not have to believe me," Marian snapped. "But it is not just my imagination." She turned her back to him and crossed her arms across her chest.

"Marian," Will spun her back to face him. "Please, do not be angry."

She sighed. "I am frustrated. Something is going on, but I have no idea what."

'Then we will solve what we can," his brown eyes stared earnestly into hers. "Little John and your mystery man first; your mother afterward."

"You are always so agreeable," Marian grumbled. "It makes it very difficult to stay mad at you."

Will grinned. "That is the point."

"How are you ever going to find a wife if all you do is wander the forest with me?" Marian was only half serious; she knew Will's heart lay in discovering what had happened to his mother at the sheriff's hands.

He shrugged and refused to meet her questioning gaze.

"You have found someone?" She knew she sounded eager, but she could not help it. This was Will, her best friend, and if he had found a measure of happiness, then she was happy, too.

"There is someone in town," he mumbled under his breath. "Can we please not talk about this? Aunt Constance doesn't know and I am not ready for her to find out."

"You have not told her? Why not?"

Her friend looked uncomfortable. "I want to find out about my mother first, that is all."

Marian squeezed Will's hand briefly before letting it go again. "I will see what I can learn at Nottingham."

"Marian, is that you?" A woman's rasping voice came from deep within the room at Will's back.

"Yes, Ms. Constance," Marian said. "I just came to ask Will a question."

"It is after dark, dear. Why are you not home and in bed?" The querulous voice continued.

Marian rolled her eyes before answering. "My mother knows I am here, Ms. Constance."

"Well, you are far too young to be out so late. I do not know what Beatrix is thinking."

"Yes, ma'am, I am about to go home now." She touched Will's arm again. His aunt had not been right in the head since his mother, Dulcina, had vanished from the castle.

"Come by tomorrow, at a more decent hour." Constance said. "Will can come out and play then."

"Good night, Mari," Will said. "Come by and play tomorrow!"

"Shhhh…" Marian stifled her laughter. "That is unkind. It is not your aunt's fault she is the way she is. Besides, I cannot come tomorrow. Mother wants to take me shopping. She claims I need more gowns."

"You do." Will shrugged when Marian wrinkled her nose at him.

"Good night, Will." Marian walked down the nearly empty street. The only people left were a few shop owners, locking their doors behind them as they left for the evening. It always amazed her how quickly the town turned silent once night fell, but she knew that would change within the next two days, as people from surrounding towns and villages gathered to celebrate May Day.

Chapter Three:

"Are you ready yet?" Mother knocked on Marian's bedroom door. "We need to leave soon if we are to purchase all our fabrics."

Marian pulled the door open. "I am ready."

Mother gasped. "Oh, no you are not." She gestured to the breeches and tunic Marian wore. "You will *not* go into town wearing those, Marian du Luc!"

"None of my gowns fit," Marian protested.

"Then we will make one fit," Mother said. "I will not allow you to disgrace our bloodlines by parading around in *those*."

"I have worn them in town before, Mother."

The look on Mother's face was implacable. "But not now. Not when everyone knows we are purchasing materials for court gowns."

"But—"

"No, Marian. Change. Now."

Marian grumbled under her breath, but did as instructed. The soft blue wool gown she chose was beautiful in its simplicity. Too bad, she thought, it does not fit. She drew in a deep breath and released it slowly once Mother had lowered it over her head.

"I. Cannot. Breathe." Marian gasped.

Mother tugged at the sleeves on the gown. "Stop exaggerating. It *is* a bit tight, but you will not faint." She bent down and helped Marian into her shoes. "There. Now you look presentable."

And uncomfortable, Marian thought but did not dare say aloud. Her breasts strained against the fabric with every short breath she took and she felt as though her ribcage was trying to escape the confines of her body.

"We shall visit the seamstress last," Mother said. "That way, we can give her all our fabric choices, fit you for all your gowns, *and* see to your final May Queen fitting." She smiled at Marian, her eyes sparkling. "It will be a fun day, Mari. You will see."

Marian was fairly sure it wouldn't be, at least not for her, but she smiled and nodded her agreement. Mother was a force of nature and once she made a decision there was no changing her mind. Whether Marian enjoyed it or not, her day would be spent looking at fabrics and being poked and prodded.

"You will need jewels, as well." Mother said, following Marian into the hall. "Be sure to include Guinvere's hair comb. Not only will it garner the proper attentions at court, but it is truly one of the loveliest pieces you own."

The instruction was unnecessary. The jeweled comb was one of Marian's treasures and she prized it highly.

"On second thought," Mother continued. "I think we shall have to purchase those ready-made gowns Vernice's shop carries. Three days will not be enough time to ensure you have the necessary gowns to make the correct impression."

"Who am I supposed to impress?" Marian huffed. "I thought we were going simply to show our support."

"Even so. There are always those at court who wish to undermine in hopes of gaining royal influence." Mother shot Marian a penetrating glance over her shoulder. "Did something happen to you in the woods?"

"Why would you ask that?" Marian stalled answering.

"You are not arguing." Mother smiled to take the sting from her words, stopped walking and turned to face her daughter. "If something happened, it is important you tell me," she said.

It was the most serious Marian had ever seen her. "No, nothing happened," she lied.

Mother nodded once. She pulled open the front door and gestured to Marian. "Oh, good, the carriage is waiting."

"Do we really need a carriage?"

"Yes, we really do. You may be used to walking into town, but I am not. And we will have too much to carry, even with Anna accompanying us."

If she could have, Marian would have sighed. While Anna was a competent maid, she was also a notorious gossip. Whatever transpired between Marian and Mother would be broadcast over every inch of town within a day. She did not understand why Mother had hired her.

"Ma'am, Marian, sorry I am late!" Anna hurried up to them, her face wreathed in smiles. "I can hardly stand it! Court!"

"Wait, what?" Marian looked at Mother in disbelief. "She is going to court with us?"

"Naturally," Mother said. "You need a ladies maid and Anna is more than capable."

The young girl turned wide green eyes on Marian. "Y-you do not want me to come?"

"No, that is not it," Marian said. "It is just—well, this whole thing is so sudden. I do not even know what court entails."

Anna sniffed. "Oh, all right. I unnerstand that."

"Anna, get into the carriage. Marian, a word with you?" Though she worded it as a request, Marian could tell it actually was anything but.

Once Anna was in the carriage, with the door shut, Mother spoke. "Marian, you will need a maid while you are at court. Not only would it be inappropriate for you to be without one, you need someone capable of doing your hair and helping you dress."

"I can *normally* dress myself," Marian stated.

"Court gowns are not similar in any way to the simple ones I have allowed you to wear here," Mother said. "They require more— attention—and care. This is not something I will discuss with you. Anna is joining us. The rest of the maids we can borrow from someone at the castle."

"Rest of the maids?" Marian said weakly. She was not sure if it was the tightness of the gown, or the idea of multiple maids that made her feel light-headed.

"Of course. There will be at least six. One maid cannot do everything, Marian. It would be unsuitable."

"Mother, I feel odd," Marian swayed as she tried to climb up into the carriage.

"Do not take such deep breaths," Mother instructed, helping Marian onto the seat next to Anna. "You are too used to breeches and tunics. When we return from Nottingham, that will change. It is past time for you to embrace your lineage and leave your childhood behind. Now, what colors do you prefer?"

Marian shrugged. "I do not know. Green, maybe? Or red?"

"Do not shrug, Marian. It is unladylike. Well, it must be the proper green," the other woman mused. "One emerald and silver, I think, and the other one red with gold shot threads. I will loan you my circlet, as well. Once your hair is done properly, it will look lovely on you."

Marian felt the carriage begin to move. "It all sounds perfect." Her eyes began to drift closed.

"Now is not the time for you to sleep, Marian!"

Marian heard Mother's voice, but it sounded as though she was speaking through a pillow and no matter how hard she tried she could not focus on what Mother was telling her.

"Marian! Marian! Anna, slap her!" Mother's instructions faded as the world around her faded and grew black.

A soft tapping on her cheek slowly penetrated her consciousness.

"Not like that!" came Mother's harsh voice and Marian heard, just for an instant, a thread of fear in it. "Move!"

The next slap rocked her head to the left and her eyes shot open. She met Mother's concerned deep blue eyes. "Marian, can you hear me?"

Marian nodded slowly. "I—what happened? Did I fall asleep?"

"You fainted, ma'am," Anna said. "I tried to wake you, but you wouldn't."

"You—hit me," Marian accused, looking at Mother. The older woman nodded. "Yes, and I would again, given the circumstances. Anna," she instructed the maid, "she needs her ties loosened. Not enough to be immodest, but enough so she can breathe."

"Yes'm."

Marian leaned away from the maid. "I can loosen my own ties," she protested, proving her words as she said them.

"You need to allow Anna to help you," Mother said.

"When we reach Nottingham, I will. But it cannot make any difference in a carriage."

Mother raised one elegant eyebrow and Marian subsided, choosing instead to change the subject.

"How long will it take us to get to the castle?" Marian asked.

"We will stop overnight at an inn halfway between town and there," Mother said. "It will take us most of two days to reach Nottingham, then another half day to get to the castle itself."

Marian bit the inside of her lip. She had hoped to see Robin again before she left, but did not know how that would be possible with the rush of the Festival.

The carriage ground to a halt.

"Feeling better?" Mother asked. She sounded genuinely concerned.

Marian took a deep breath in and slowly released it. "Yes," she said.

"Then let us get you clothing which actually fits," Mother smiled. "Anna, if you would..."

The small maid rose from her seat and opened the door, waiting until both Marian and Mother stepped down and onto the road before joining them.

Mother looked critically at Marian. "Vernice's shop first," she said. "We *must* get you out of that gown and into something more fashionable."

It was as though the woman who had slapped her awake did not exist anymore, Marian thought. That idea stayed with her throughout the day, as she was fitted for gown after gown after gown. It was not until they were on their way home, Anna loaded down with new gowns of every shade and variety, that she brought up what was really bothering her.

"Why have you never taken me to court before now?"

"Marian, this is not the proper time to speak of such things." Mother said.

"It is *never* the proper time!" Marian objected.

19

"You and I will speak of this later." Mother's eyes flicked to Anna, who was listening, eyes wide.

Marian's mouth snapped shut, too late. By the same time tomorrow, the entire town would know of the arguments between her and Mother. She had not been thinking of the consequences when she spoke.

"The gowns look lovely on you," Mother said. "I am especially pleased with the royal blue one. I think that is the one you shall wear to supper once we arrive."

Marian began to shrug, but stopped halfway through at Mother's glare.

"May I go into Sherwood when we get back?" She asked.

Mother sighed. "You know I would prefer you stayed out of those woods," she began. "But yes. As long as you come back before dusk."

The sun had just topped the highest building in town. Marian figured she had enough time to explore and possibly meet Robin again.

"Take Will with you," Mother continued, and Marian's heart dropped.

"I will wear my sword," she bargained. "Aunt Constance was having a –bad—day when I saw Will last night. I doubt he will be able to leave her."

"Poor Constance," Mother said. "First losing her brother to the sheriff's men, then her sister-in-law vanishing like that... it is no wonder she has lost her mind." She changed her tactic. "Anna can go with you instead."

The young girl began shaking her head. "Oh, no, ma'am. I am sorry, but I cannot. I just cannot."

Both Marian and Mother raised their eyebrows at the terror in her voice.

"What is the matter?" Marian asked.

"It is the—the woods. All those trees n' all. I cannot go in there!"

"All right," Mother soothed. "You do not have to go. It will be all right, Anna."

Marian gave a sigh of relief. Anna's fear meant she would be going into the woods alone, just as she wished.

"Of course," Mother continued, "you realize this means you cannot go into the woods today."

"What? Why not?" Marian demanded.

"We had this discussion already, Marian. You violated our agreement. I obviously cannot trust you in the woods alone. Since no-one can attend you today, it stands to reason you may not go."

Marian's jaw tightened. "I will ask Father," she said.

"Please do," Mother said calmly, "if you believe it will serve your purposes." She waited until the carriage slowed to a halt. "Anna, take those gowns into Marian's room and place them across her bed. They need to be aired before they are packed."

"Yes, ma'am." Anna gathered the gowns into her arms. The carriage door opened, one of their footmen holding the door, waiting for the women to descend.

"Marian, before you defy me, do me the favor of changing your gown. That old one has plenty of life left in it; put it into the hall basket to be donated." Mother commented. "Anna can help you into one of the simpler ones we bought."

Marian shrugged, too angry to respond. She strode toward the house, Anna hurrying along behind.

"She is too insufferable for words," Marian's violet linen gown bunched up under her as she leaned forward and rested her elbows on Father's desk. "All she ever thinks about is our lineage and my possible marriage prospects."

Father dipped his quill into his inkwell. "You broke the single restriction she placed on you, Marian." The quill scratched across the surface of the parchment in front of him. "What reaction did you expect from her?"

"It is the one place I feel like I belong," she protested. "I do not know why she refuses to understand that!"

Father stopped writing and leaned back in his chair. "Oh, she understands more than she lets you know," he said. "You two are very alike, after all."

"I doubt that," Marian said. "And now she is starting to act...oddly. It almost seems like she is two different people."

Father laughed. "Your mother is exactly who she has always been, Mari. No more, no less." He reached over his shoulder with one hand and grabbed a parchment from one of the wooden shelves behind him; shelves that were stacked tall with bound papers of every size.

"She is obviously keeping secrets," Marian tried again. "Why does that not bother you?"

Father spread the parchment in front of him, holding it flat in one hand as he took the quill from the inkwell with the other. "Any secrets your mother has are hers to keep. I trust her."

"It was one mistake, Father," Marian said. "Why will she not see that and trust me to not make it again?"

"Tell me, Marian, why are you so impatient to go back into Sherwood? Her restriction was until after the Festival, and that is only two days away."

Marian bit her lip, considering her reply. "I met someone," she finally admitted. "And I would like to see him again."

"Ah." Father laid the quill softly across the parchment, and leaned back again, lacing his long fingers behind his head. "And who is this mysterious 'someone', Mari?"

"His name is Robin," she said. "He lives in the forest and is loyal to King Richard."

"You know this because he has told you so?" Father raised one eyebrow.

Marian flushed. "Well...yes."

"I have met your Robin," Father admitted. He held up one hand to stop her from speaking. "He has helped keep me safe when I travel through Sherwood."

"Then you know what he is like," Marian chattered. "You can talk some sense into Mother!"

Father shook his head. "No. Your mother has her reasons for doing what she is doing. I will not interfere."

"So that is all? Even though you know Robin, you will not do anything?"

"I do not have time for this, Marian. I need to get this music written before the Festival." He began singing under his breath in a low velvet baritone.

Marian rose to her feet. Once Father started singing, the conversation was over and nothing she said would make any difference.

The singing broke off. "Wait a moment." He pushed away from his desk and opened one of the drawers. "I was saving this for a special occasion," he began, "but now seems as good a time as any." He held a stack of papers in his hand. "I wrote these for you. One per year since the day of your birth."

"What are they?" Marian asked.

"Ballads," Father answered. "Your history put to music."

Tears filled Marian's eyes. "You turned my life into music?"

Father smiled gently. "I was only returning the favor."

"I love you, Father."

"I love you, too, Mari. Now off with you, so I can write."

Marian clutched the sheave of papers in one hand as she closed the door behind her with the other. She would read Father's ballads in her room. It was not a bad way to spend the remainder of her day.

Chapter Four:

Marian straightened the garland of flowers sliding down over one ear and shifted uncomfortably on the wooden platform. The morning smelled of cherry blossoms, which drowned out the more ordinary scent of horses, hay, and trampled dirt.

"Marian, Marian, watch me!"

The boys from town and beyond held impromptu races, each one trying in vain to capture her attention. As May Queen, it was her duty to reward the winners of every competition. The sun had barely risen and already she could feel the sweat dripping down the back of her neck. The white gown she wore tangled around her legs as she shifted again.

"Stop fidgeting," Mother said from her seat just below Marian. "You will tear the embroidery."

Marian glanced down at her gown. The bell-like sleeves, hem and bodice were banded in little deep blue forget-me-nots and thin silver thread. The seamstress had done a beautiful job.

"It is time for the blessing. Marian, I know you never wanted to be the Queen, but you need to do your job." Mother said. "No man likes a woman who refuses to behave properly."

Marian hid a smile, thinking of Robin. He seemed to like her just the way she was. "I know what my duties are," she said. "I will perform them to the best of my ability."

Mother smiled. "That is my girl." She walked away.

Stretching out her right hand, palm toward the ground, Marian spoke the traditional words. "I give you God's blessing and pray a bounty over your fields and hearths."

No sooner had she finished speaking than the crowd scattered, each to their chosen contests. The footraces held little interest for her, and the official sword fighting contests wouldn't take place until later in the day. She turned her attention instead to the archery contest, where young men raised bows to cheeks and waited to let the arrows fly toward the bales of hay stacked three and four high in a nearby field. Robin had not promised her he would come; he had not promised her anything, but she could not stop the hope that rose in her breast. Marian searched the rows of archers without success. Most of the men had their hoods pulled up against the early morning chill. She sighed and dropped the white handkerchief she held, signaling the official beginning of the festival.

The twanging of bows carried up to where she sat; swords rang, and cheers resounded. As the footraces began Marian yawned and sat back down. Almost immediately loud clapping drew her attention back to where the archers stood. A lone archer, his hood drawn up, drew back his arm, fit arrow to string, and released it in one swift movement, then repeated the process almost faster than her eyes could follow. The arrows blurred in flight, burying themselves in the center of the farthest hay bale. The other contestants clapped him good-naturedly on the shoulder. The archer simply nodded as he collected his own arrows and returned them to his quiver before approaching Marian.

"I am here to collect my reward for winning the tournament," the mocking voice caught at her heartstrings.

Marian licked her lips nervously as she stared into familiar gray eyes. The fluttering begun in her heart migrated to her stomach, threatening to give birth to full-grown butterflies. She searched desperately for something to say. "Why are you here?"

Robin raised one red-brown eyebrow. "To collect my reward…it was advertised as a kiss from the May Queen herself." He leaned toward her. "Are you going to deny me my well deserved reward, Maid Marian?"

"Robin, there are other contests with greater rewards than this one," she murmured.

His breath was a tiny puff of air against her lips. "I cannot imagine a greater prize than the one I am about to collect." His lips lightly brushed against hers, and she felt the butterflies in her stomach take flight. "You have not been to Sherwood in a few days," he continued.

"You—you noticed?" Marian stuttered. His lips were still inches from her own and each word he spoke sent shivers up her spine.

"Of course," he said. "I keep track of everything that happens in my woods."

"You mean King Richard's woods," Marian corrected.

Robin laughed. "Are you always so literal?"

"The woods do not belong to you," she said.

"Well, technically, they do not belong to the king, either," Robin said. "The woods were there long before Richard came to the throne."

"Do not tell me they belong to the fairies," Marian said, remembering Will's insistence about winged creatures deep in the forest.

Robin grinned. "Who told you about the fairies?"

Marian barely stopped herself from shrugging. "Will Scarlett," she said.

"Will should stop listening to rumors. When can you come back to Sherwood, Marian? I would love to learn more about how you became such a *literal*, sword wielding girl." He winked.

"I am unsure," she hated to say the words. "Our family has been summoned to Nottingham Castle. We leave within the week."

Robin's eyes narrowed. "Why?"

"I am...we are... descendants of the throne," she said. "It is ancient history, but Mother insists we have to go to prove our loyalty."

"Your loyalty to Prince John?" His voice was flat.

Marian shook her head. "No, our loyalty to the throne."

"Prince John will not see it that way," he said. He leaned forward. "Is this the only contest with the reward I collected, or are there more, waiting for the same sweetness I just tasted?"

Marian blushed, a deep red that infused her cream colored skin. "N—no, this is—was the only one."

He laughed. "If you can get away when this Festival is over, come into the forest." When she started to shake her head, he continued.

"You are not leaving for the castle tonight. Are you willing to spare me a few paltry hours?"

"I have to be home before the sun sets," she said a bit nervously.

"I will make sure you are home before anyone finds out you have gone," he grinned. He reached out and took her hand in his. "'Til later, my sweet Marian." Pressing the lightest of kisses against the palm of her hand, he stepped backward, turned and vanished into crowds surrounding the archery circle.

"Who was that?" Mother asked curiously, climbing up to where Marian sat with a meat pie in her hand. "I brought you something to eat."

"Thank you." Marian accepted the pie from Mother and bit into it eagerly. The seasoned beef and potatoes tasted heavenly.

"So are you going to answer my question?" Mother seated herself next to Marian.

"He was just the archer who won the contest," Marian said.

"It seemed to be more than that. You were speaking to him for some time."

"He was curious how I became the May Queen. That is all." Lying to Mother was becoming easier each time she did it. She took another bite of the pie. "Do you need my help with anything after the Festival?"

"No, and I know you are itching to go into the woods. Just do not stay too late, and be sure to take your sword."

It was Marian's turn to raise a blond eyebrow. "You are letting me go?"

"We shall be in Nottingham shortly. I know how much Sherwood Forest means to you. You should take the opportunity to walk them before we leave."

Marian's eyes sparkled briefly before she frowned. "But the Festival does not end until nearly sundown. That will not give me much time."

"Take Will with you. I saw him speaking to Betsy over by the pie cart."

"I will go speak to him now," Marian said. There would be more prizes to hand out, though none of them was a kiss from her. That was always reserved for the best archer, though she was not sure why.

"Be careful of your gown, Marian!" Mother admonished.

One hand held her skirts off the ground as Marian hurried in Will's direction.

"Marian, nice of you to join us," Betsy, the young woman standing next to Will, spoke first. "Are your duties as the Queen done, then?"

Marian shook her head. "No, I still have a few more," she said. "Festival has barely begun."

Will cocked an eyebrow at her. "Then what are you doing here?"

"I needed to speak to you," she said. She cast a glance at Betsy, who stared back. "But it can wait."

"That is all right. Will, I shall see you tomorrow?" Betsy smirked at Marian, who did not react.

"Yes, of course," Will said. "As planned. I will come by after breakfast." He waited until she left before turning toward Marian. "What happened?"

"That is her, isn't it?" Marian asked. "The one you are interested in."

Will shook his head, but the denial came too quickly.

"She *is*."

"Never mind her. Tell me what happened," he demanded again.

Marian lowered her voice. "I saw him."

Her friend frowned. "Who?"

"Him," Marian said. "*Him*. The one I told you about; Robin. He was here. He won the archery contest." She flushed again, thinking of Robin's lips on hers. "Were you not watching?"

"All I saw was an archer with his hood pulled up," Will said. "What did he want?"

"He wants me to meet him in Sherwood. Tonight."

"You have not changed your mind about coming to the meeting with Little John?" Will asked.

Marian shook her head. "But you know what is strange about the whole thing? Mother is encouraging it."

"I am not following you," Will frowned. "You mean your mother is allowing you to meet a stranger in the woods?"

"No, of course not. She does not know anything about that. She is letting me into Sherwood past sunset. Provided you are with me. So if she mentions it to you, tell her you agreed."

Will shrugged. "It is nothing more than the truth. More or less."

"I will not have time to change," Marian spoke, almost to herself. "And mother told me to bring my sword. Will you go and bring it back for me? It is on the hook on the backside of my door."

"I will get it," Will promised. "I will meet you by the—" he glanced around, "the blacksmith."

Marian agreed and they parted ways once more.

The remainder of the Festival bored Marian and she found herself daydreaming of Robin; of the way his hair would fall through her fingers in a cascade of color. His eyes would stare deeply into hers as he leaned forward to kiss her. A tiny smile played about her lips.

"Marian du Luc, do you hear a word I am saying?"

Marian's eyes snapped open to see Mother staring at her.

"I...no," she admitted ruefully. Behind Mother stood a burly man, sweat staining his shirt and sword sheathed at his side.

"This is the winner of the sword tournament," Mother continued. "He is awaiting his reward from his Queen." She glared and Marian flinched. "I *told* him you were deeply impressed by his feat," she hissed under her breath. "Act the part."

"My Lord," Marian said, holding out her hand to the man. "You are brave beyond all words." Mother handed a small bag to Marian, and she, in turn, gave it to her 'knight'. "Take this reward as a small token of my eternal thanks."

"Thank y', M'Queen." The man said, releasing Marian's hand to take the small bag of coins from her. "Y're most kind."

Marian expected Mother to lecture her once the man turned away. Instead, she was surprised when Mother simply said, "The Festival is over. You have daydreamed most of it away. You are welcome to leave at any time."

Marian blinked, looking around her more closely. Most of the people had long since gone home and only the usual townsmen were left.

She walked off the platform and through the remainder of the Festival. The smithy was just outside the town limits and its back was mere feet from her favorite path into Sherwood.

Chapter Five:

"Does Betsy know you are here?" Marian greeted Will.

Will nodded ruefully. "I could not lie to her about it."

Marian took her sword from him and buckled it around her waist. "I do not care for her," she said bluntly.

"She is not for you to like or dislike," Will stated. "*I* like her. And she does not normally behave that way. She does not understand our friendship, that is all."

"How long have you been keeping her secret?" Marian asked.

"A few months," Will said. "It is nothing serious."

"She seemed terribly serious about you," Marian disagreed.

"As I said before, I am *not* contemplating marriage until I know what happened to my mother. Can we just drop the subject?" His voice was strained. "I will explain tonight to her later."

"As you like." Marian gestured towards the path behind the smithy. "Are you ready?"

"As much as I can be," Will returned. "Remember to stay out of sight. I do not want Little John knowing I did not come alone."

Marian and Will skirted the inner forest. The darkened trees looked inviting, the branches green and heavy with moss, and Marian slipped off the path to blend, as best as she could in her Festival gown, among them. Tiny drops of sweat beaded her forehead and she brushed them away. She drew in a deep breath, letting the fresh woodland smells permeate her senses. Releasing the air slowly, she let her mind drift. Once Will met with Little John, she would be free to meet Robin, though she was not sure how he would find her.

"Yuh came."

The voice was all the warning she had to flatten herself behind the closest tree trunk and peer out around it.

"I did," Will told Little John. "What did you want to talk to me about?"

The huge man scratched at his beard. "Why, joinin' us, of course."

"Who's 'us'?" Will leaned casually against the same tree Marian hid behind and she ducked back to keep from being seen.

"The Merry Men," Little John said. "Who else?"

"Are you Hood?"

Little John laughed. "C'n yuh just see me, as Hood?!"

Marian peeked back out. If Little John was not Hood…who was?

"Is he here?" Will persisted. "I will not join an outlaw band without speaking to its leader first."

"Then we have a problem," Little John said. "Hood does not show himself to anyone excep' his Merry Men. He calls it self-…self preserv…preserv…"

"Preservation, Little John," said the last voice Marian expected to hear. "It is called self preservation." Robin stepped through the trees.

Marian gasped, and Robin's eyes narrowed. "We have company," he said. He pointed to where Marian was hiding. "There, behind that tree. Grab him."

Arms pulled Marian away from the tree trunk and hauled her into the clearing.

Robin's eyebrows crawled into his hairline. "Well, well, if it is not my sweet Maid Marian. Will Scarlett, I do believe this changes things. You and I will speak later. Marian, what are you doing here?"

Marian shook free of the arms holding her. "I came to meet you! I just did not know who you really were!"

"I am exactly who I told you I am. Robin."

"Robin *Hood*," Marian folded her arms across her chest. "And you never said a word."

Robin shrugged. "You never asked."

"You *knew* I wanted to join Hood's band!"

"You never told me that," Robin snapped back.

"It was implied!" Marian clenched her jaw.

It was Robin's turn to cross his arms. "That," he said emphatically, "will never happen."

Marian uncrossed her arms and took two steps forward on the grass. "Why not?"

"You are a girl," Robin said. "It is too dangerous."

Squirrels scurried through the undergrowth as Marian drew in a breath and released it slowly. Will stepped backward, joining the slowly gathering circle of men around Robin and Marian.

"I can handle myself," Marian finally retorted. "I have my sword." Her hand fell to its pommel.

Robin laughed. "You expect to use that old thing? Have you even *looked* at it closely? It is a hand and a half too long and ancient. Why, the last arming sword I saw was over six hundred years old! Does it even hold its edge?"

The sword almost leapt of its own accord into Marian's hand as she drew it from the sheath. "It holds its edge just fine," she said. "And I know how to use it. Little John did not tell you?"

"Knowing how to hold a sword is different from using one, sweet maid." Robin stretched out his hand. The tall blond man who had whisked Marian from her hiding place drew his own longsword and held it out. "If you can best me, I will *consider* allowing you to join us," Robin promised, taking the blade from Trent.

"Agreed," Marian said. She began circling to keep the shafts of sunlight from her eyes. Her foot tangled in the hem of her gown and before she could regain her footing, Robin's sword plunged toward her. Her sword met his in a clash that sent waves of pain resonating up her arm. Her fingers loosened, but the blade stayed molded to her palm.

Fighting back involuntary tears, she looked up to see Robin's hand extended towards her. She shoved her hair away from her face and winced as he pulled her to her feet.

"Had enough?"

Marian shook her head and pushed him back. "We have only begun, unless you fear being beaten by a girl."

Trent and the others laughed good-naturedly. Cries of 'Get 'er, Robin!' and 'She is jus' a girl," filled the clearing.

Robin chuckled at her audacity. "No, maid Marian, I do not fear losing to you and your prized sword. I simply do not want to injure you… or your misplaced pride in your abilities."

Marian knew she should not rise to the bait, but she did. "My pride is hardly misplaced," she ground out. She thrust toward him without warning; he parried, knocking her sword away time and time again, until they were both dripping with sweat.

"Are you sure you would not prefer to just give up?" Robin grinned. "You look tired." He swung his sword unexpectedly and Marian barely got her sword up in time. "I thought you said you were good," he taunted.

"I am," she panted. "You have not won."

"Yet." He thrust again and this time her sword met his with a resounding crash.

"Robin of Locksley, just what in the world do you think you are doing?"

A clear, crisp voice rang through the clearing. Marian, startled, dropped her guard for a split second. Robin's longsword slid underneath to nick her upper arm.

"Damn it," the words slipped out before she could restrain herself and the men erupted into raucous laughter and clapping.

Robin winked at her, wiping the sword on his sleeve before returning it to Trent.

"Whose voice was that?" Marian sheathed her blade.

"Mine." The trees rustled and an old woman, white hair hanging down to her waist, stepped into the clearing. "Robin, what are you doing here?"

"I live here, you know that," Robin said blandly.

"Do not test me, boy," the old woman glared. "You are meddling in things best left alone."

"But…who *are* you?" Marian asked again.

The old woman straightened. "I am Nottingham's historian. I keep track of *everything* that happens; both here and at the castle."

"She is an interfering old lady," Robin, crossing the space between himself and the other woman, drew her into a quick embrace. "It is good to see you, Nyneve."

"You hush," the woman pretended to be upset, but Marian could see the twinkle in her eyes as she looked at Robin.

"What sorts of things is he meddling in?" Marian asked.

A pair of deep gray eyes pierced Marian. They made her feel like a bug she had once seen cut in half with a knife. The old woman glanced down at the sheathed sword, then back up to Marian's face. "You are a curious girl. Robin, you and I have things to discuss. Girl, you need to return home. I know of your mother, and she would be most concerned if you stayed out much longer. The moon has long since topped the trees."

How the old woman could tell, Marian did not know. They were deep enough in the woods that the sky was no longer visible.

"Why are you still here?" The other woman snapped and Marian did not wait to hear anymore. There was something about the old woman, like an irritable spider in the middle of a massive web, which made Marian not want to risk her possible wrath. She left Will there and ran.

Chapter Six:

The knock at her door roused Marian from dreams filled with Robin; dreams of him drawing her close and holding her in his arms; kissing her, confessing his love to her.

"Marian, you have overslept," Mother's scolding tone came through the door. "Our escort has arrived and is impatient to leave. A gown has already been laid out on your chair."

Marian swung her legs over the side of the bed and looked around. The dress Mother had chosen was a concoction of light green cotton and lace. It was hideous, but very fashionable. She reluctantly picked it up and dropped the soft folds over her head, pulling the front laces shut and tying them.

"Marian," This time it was Father's voice she heard.

"Yes, Father, I am coming." Marian smoothed her hair down with her hairbrush and drew it into a low knot on her neck. Glancing at her herself in the small mirror on her bedside table, she shrugged at her warped reflection. She was as presentable as she was going to be.

"Hmm," was all Mother said when Marian walked out. "Maybe that color was not the best choice, but there is no changing it now. Go with your father. I have sent Anna into town for a few last minute things. I will wait here."

Marian followed Father through the house and into the courtyard. The hard packed dirt stirred under the hooves of six horses, each bearing a rider dressed in identical black leather with blue trim.

"The sheriff did not want to take any chances with outlaws," Father said. "His men are here to ensure we arrive safely."

"The outlaws would not hurt us," Marian said.

"I am not referring to Hood's Merry Men, but bandits."

"Do I have time to visit Will before we leave?" Marian asked.

Father shook his head. "No."

"But I need to make sure he is…" she trailed off.

"He is fine," Father said.

Marian sneezed. "How do you know?"

"He came by while you were still asleep. He asked me to make sure you knew he had gotten home safe." Father's eyes narrowed. "Is there something I should be worried about?"

Marian shook her head. "No." She did not know how to explain what had happened with the strange old woman to Father, and definitely did not want him to know about Robin being Hood.

A man stepped forward from his waiting place beside one of two carriages. "You must be Alan a Dale and the Lady Marian. I am Roger de Lacy, the Sheriff of Nottingham. It is my pleasure to meet you."

He did not look like the man who had ordered the death of Will's father. He towered over Marian, muscular without being overweight, and with short, neatly trimmed brown hair and light brown eyes.

Taking her hand in his, he bowed over it, barely brushing its surface with his lips. "I have heard much about your—family. It is an interesting history."

"It is ancient history," Marian retorted. "It has no bearing on who we are now."

"Nonetheless," he murmured, almost to himself, "it is a royal lineage." He released her hand. "Speaking of royalty, where is your lovely mother? I was informed she would be joining us."

"She was unavoidably detained," Father inserted smoothly. "I am sure she will be here soon."

The sheriff drummed his fingers against the side of the closest carriage, while the men on the horses continued to mill around the courtyard. "I would prefer to leave as soon as possible."

Father's voice hardened. "I said she will be here, Sheriff."

"Will it take long to reach the castle?" Marian asked in a vain attempt to change the subject.

"If we do not leave soon, we will not reach the inn before nightfall," the tall man continued. "Travel through Sherwood can be—problematic—after dark."

"Have you been having difficulty with bandits?" Marian asked. Even knowing how evil the sheriff was, her breath caught in his presence. His face was slender, the cheekbones angular under skin tanned brown from the sun. He was handsome. Not at all like Robin, with his mane of red-gold and brown hair. This man was polished. Refined.

He scowled his reply and glared at the offending forest. "Not bandits. *Outlaws*. If they did not have somewhere to hide, we could find and hang them all."

Marian gasped. "Hang them?" She stared at him, and suddenly found his face repulsive instead of handsome. The lovely brown eyes were not soft, but hard as the rocks beneath her shoes, and his lips were thin with potential cruelty.

"They are dangerous to everyone." He turned to Father. "Surely you have had your own problems here?"

"No, we have not," Father said.

A door closed and Mother, Anna hurrying behind her, swayed across the courtyard. "Sheriff, it has been too long." She held out one hand and the sheriff kissed it briefly before releasing it. "Anna, put the packages into the sheriff's carriage. I am sure he will not mind."

"Of course not," the sheriff said. "Anything I can do to help, I will."

"Very kind of you," Mother said. "The footmen should be bringing our chests out shortly."

The sheriff smiled at Mother, but it never quite reached his eyes. "It would be my very great honor to have the luxury of Marian's company on the trip to Nottingham."

Marian's eyes widened. It was a wholly inappropriate request.

"Absolutely not," Father snapped. "It is out of the question. Her integrity would be compromised beyond all recovery." He put one restraining hand on Mother's arm. "We could not allow it."

"She is such a lovely girl," the sheriff said blandly, "I thought I could entertain her with tales of the castle before she sees it for the first time. She could, of course, bring her servant."

"Maid," Mother corrected. "We do not have servants here."

"Of course," the sheriff agreed. "My apologies to you both."

"Anna, help Marian into the carriage," Mother instructed. "Sheriff, we will see you at the inn."

The sheriff looked startled to be so quickly dismissed, but he bowed one last time. "Very well. Do you object to my leaving some men here, to ensure your safety until you leave?"

"Of course not," Mother said. She ran her hands down her blue silk gown to smooth the fabric. "We would be most pleased to have you looking after our interests."

Marian clambered into the carriage, Anna's hand at her elbow.

"He is handsome, ain't he?" Anna seated herself across from Marian. "The stories I have heard sure did not lie."

Before Marian could answer, the carriage rocked slightly as the footmen outside tied down chests and boxes.

"I mean, look at him," Anna continued. "And they say he is close to the prince."

"He is rumored to be Prince John's closest friend," Marian agreed. Thankfully, she was spared more of her maid's chatter by her parents. Mother seated herself next to Marian, arranging her gown carefully. Father took the seat next to Anna, his long legs stretching out and his boots resting on the floor by Marian's feet.

"Is he gone?" Marian asked.

"Not yet," Father said. "He is giving his men some last minute instructions. We have a few more things that need to be loaded before we leave. Beatrix, did you tell the footmen to bring the brass banded oak chest?"

Mother nodded. "It was the first one they loaded on."

"What is in the oak chest?" Marian's curiosity was piqued.

Mother and Father shared a long look before Mother answered. "It carries a few important sundries I might require."

It was apparent that was the only answer she was going to receive.

The thundering of hooves heralded the sheriff's leaving at the same time the carriage rocked on its wheels again.

"*Now* we can leave," Father said, thumping the roof of the coach. The carriage lurched forward as the horses found their rhythm, then settled into a steady rocking motion.

"It is a full day's travel to the castle," Mother said, answering Marian's earlier question. "It would be too much to attempt in a single day, and we will need to eat, as well as let the horses rest. The inn the sheriff referred to is safe from outlaws. Even they respect the owner."

"Who's that?" Marian asked.

"King Richard," Mother said. "He had the inn built after one of his horses went lame while he was hunting."

Marian stared out the window. Once the carriage entered Sherwood Forest, all she saw were oak trees lining either side of the dirt road. While she loved the forest, she preferred walking the leaf strewn paths to riding on the main road. She sighed and closed her eyes. Her dreams had been full of elaborately gowned men and women, dancing in circles around her, laughing, while Robin and the strange lady from the forest sat in a spider's web, watching. Needless to say, her sleep had not been restful. She dozed off.

The utter stillness of the carriage woke her a short time later.

"Are we at the inn already?" Marian asked, rubbing her eyes. Anna sat with her eyes shut, mouth open as she snored lightly. Father stuck his head out the window. "Why have we stopped?" There was a low murmur of voices. Father turned to Mother. "The sheriff's men found a poacher's trap not far from here. He has decided to take matters into his own hands."

Mother grimaced. "Killing men in the prince's name will *not* endear him to the king when he returns."

"You know as well as I do that the sheriff's not interested in the king's opinion of him," Father said.

"He is going to kill someone while we just wait here?" Marian blanched. "Should we not do something?"

"What would you propose?" Mother's voice was flat.

"If I had my sword," Marian began.

"You would only get yourself killed." Mother finished. She fanned her face with one hand. "You have no idea how cruel those poachers can be!"

"They are hungry, Mother. I hardly think that makes them brutal murderers."

"You have never gone without," Father interrupted. "Men in adverse conditions will do anything to survive."

"It is unnecessarily cruel," Marian said. "There's plenty of game in the forest for everyone."

"It is because of the Poacher's Law," Father said. "Richard intended it to protect travelers. Prince John and the sheriff bent it for their own purpose."

Mother raised one eyebrow at Father's response. "Alan, I doubt Marian is interested in such details."

There was a hard knock at the carriage door. Anna, startled awake, sat up. "Why did we stop?" Mother glared at her and she swallowed. "I mean... are we there, ma'am?"

"Open the door," Mother directed.

Anna swung the door open and one of the sheriff's riders stood there. "The sheriff wants you to go on to the inn. He said we are to escort you, and he will meet you there later."

Mother nodded. "Thank you for escorting us and keeping us safe."

The rider nodded without further comment. At Mother's nod, Anna leaned forward, reaching for the door handle. The sheriff's man watched her for a moment before pushing the door shut himself. Almost as soon as it snicked closed, the carriage began moving once more.

"Do you really think he will kill that poacher?" Marian asked.

"If he can catch him," Father said. "You know how large Sherwood is. Chances are good the poacher will escape his fate."

"I hope so," Marian said. She leaned toward the window and looked out. The trees were denser and the underbrush looked wilder, the deeper into the forest they traveled. Part of her watched the trees in vain, hoping to catch a glimpse of Robin, or even Little John. Someone who would make her feel safe on her journey to the castle.

Chapter Seven:

The inn was larger than Marian thought it would be. It spread across the clearing; a single main building with what appeared to be stables on either side of it. The inn itself was brightly lit and inviting, the double doors opened wide.

"I see we managed to make it here before the sheriff," Mother glanced out the carriage window.

"I wish I never had to see him again," Marian said.

"That is not an option," Mother said. "He is the confidant of the prince. Anna, I need my oak chest, you know the one."

The maid nodded. "Yes, ma'am, I do. But, ma'am, it is too long for me to carry by meself."

Mother sighed. "Have one of the footmen to carry it up to our rooms."

"Ma'am, do we have rooms yet?" Anna questioned.

"Not if you stay here questioning me," Mother ground out.

"Oh, yes, ma'am, I mean, no, ma'am." The tiny maid squeaked. She clambered out of the carriage, leaving the door swinging open.

"Good grief," Mother said. "Maybe Anna was not the best choice for a ladies maid. Well, it is too late to change things now. Come. We all need to freshen up before dinner."

They exited the carriage and crossed the hard packed dirt to the open doors.

"Lady Beatrix, Alan, Marian, I am so glad you made it." The sheriff met them as soon as they crossed the threshold.

"Your men ensured we were perfectly safe," Mother responded, sweeping past him to the long wooden counter.

"I have already arranged rooms for you," the sheriff said, following behind her. "And entertainments for tonight's supper."

"I thought we would eat in our rooms after the long journey," Mother turned to face him.

The sheriff made a moue of disappointment. "But everyone is expecting the famous Alan a Dale to sing."

Mother raised an eyebrow. "Did you bother asking my husband what his wishes in this matter are?"

He narrowed his eyes, but before he could say anything, Father stepped up to Mother's side. "It is all right, Bea. This would be the perfect audience for the ballad I plan to present to His Highness."

Marian yawned behind her hand. "Would it be all right," she asked quietly, "if I had supper in my room? I am quite tired and I have heard Father sing before."

Mother nodded. "That would be acceptable."

The sheriff grimaced. "Your presence will be sorely missed," he said.

Marian stared at the floor, not wanting to meet the sheriff's eyes.

Anna, weighed down with a chest Marian recognized as hers, struggled in through the still open doors. Marian stepped forward, but Mother stopped her with a glance and a slight shake of her head. Leaning forward, she whispered in Marian's ear.

"We are royalty, and we do not assist the help. Ever."

A footman, carrying a smaller chest, stopped Anna and silently exchanged his package for hers. She smiled at him and the two of them walked toward the set of wooden stairs.

"Go on up," Father said. "We will see you in the morning."

Marian followed in Anna's footsteps, arriving at an already opened door. Through the doorway she could see her maid, filling a washbasin from a cracked and worn pitcher.

"I poured you some water to wash up before supper," Anna said.

"Thank you," Marian returned, stepping inside. "But I will not be going down for supper. I am tired and wish to stay here." She noticed Anna's slight frown. "But you can go."

Anna shook her head. "Oh, no, ma'am. That would not be proper, 'n your mother would be very upset if I left you alone."

"I will be sure to bolt the door," Marian promised, "and I will hear your knock when you come up."

"Well..." Anna hesitated for a moment. "If you insist."

"I do." She yawned again. "I really *am* tired."

"Your nightgown is packed right on top," Anna said, edging toward the door.

"I will be fine." To prove her point, Marian walked over to the chest and opened it. Pulling out the nightgown, she held it up. "See, you can tell Mother you left me getting ready for bed."

"Thank you, ma'am." Anna flashed a smile and left.

Marian promptly dropped the nightgown on the bed and sat down. Through the thin walls she could hear Father tuning his lute. It was a comforting sound.

"Hsst...Marian."

She gasped at the barely heard voice outside the window. "Robin, what are you doing here?" Marian hurried over to the window and leaned out.

He sat comfortably on a tree limb, blending into the leaves so well she could barely see him. "I had to make sure you were safe," he replied.

"Are you not aware of the price the sheriff has on your head?" She gestured him inside.

Robin shrugged. "He has not caught me yet." He threw one leg over the windowsill and levered himself into the room.

Marian's heart began to pound. "This is not proper."

Robin half smiled. "You are the one who invited me inside," he said. He stepped toward her. "And do you really care about what is 'proper'?"

She shook her head, not sure her voice would work with him standing so close.

He grinned. "Marian du Luc, you are everything I hoped for and nothing like I thought you would be."

Marian's eyes narrowed. "Your words tell me you have known of my presence for a while. How long have you been watching me in the forest?"

Robin shrugged. "I came back from the Holy Land two years ago and was banished from my father's lands shortly thereafter. While

Sherwood Forest is fascinating, I found the travelers and wanderers in it much more so." He took her hands in his. "Do you not agree?"

She blushed.

"I brought something for you," he continued. "Shut your eyes."

Marian obediently closed her eyes. Robin let go of her hands and a few moments later, a twisted and rough object was placed in them. The sweet scent of dogwood blossoms filled the small room.

"Robin, where on earth did you find this?" Marian's eyes flew open and she looked down at the stick of dogwood in her hands. "'It is not the right season for dogwood blossoms!"

He winked. "The fairies gave it to me."

"They are beautiful," she said. "But how did you know they are my favorite flower?"

"As I said, I have been watching you a long time."

"I am unsure whether to be frightened or flattered." Marian raised the dogwood to her nose and breathed in deep, enjoying the feel of the soft petals brushing against her cheeks.

"Marian," the caress of her name on his lips made her heart take flight. "You never have to be frightened of me." He stepped closer. "I will always keep you safe."

Marian lowered the dogwood and sighed. "But I am frightened, Robin. I have no idea what to expect at the castle and the sheriff is..." her voice trailed off as she considered her words. "He is frighteningly attentive."

"He has good taste," Robin murmured. He caught and held her glance. "I do not have much time," Robin said, "if I am to reach Nottingham before you."

Marian raised her eyebrows. "You shall be at the castle?"

He laughed. "While I am sure I would be a welcome...guest...in Prince John's dungeons, I have no intention of accepting his many invitations. No, I will remain close by in the forest instead." A sly grin crossed his face. "Though I would be remiss if I left without collecting my rightly earned Festival kiss."

Marian blushed again. "I—I thought you did that already," she stuttered.

He took the dogwood branch from her loosened fingers and tossed it onto the bedding. "That was merely a taste," he pulled her toward him. "What I prefer is a sampling."

Marian's breath caught in her throat. Robin leaned down, his mouth inches from capturing her own. "This is not proper, either," he whispered. "But you do not care about propriety, do you, Marian?"

She could not think with his lips so close. "I am—not sure," she finally whispered back.

One of his hands reached up to caress her cheek. "Good." He lowered his mouth purposefully.

Her eyes slid shut at the feel of his lips on hers, the stubble on his upper lip scratching her.

The knock at the door startled both of them and they leapt apart.

Chapter Eight:

"I—who is it?" Marian's voice shook.

"Marian, what is wrong?" The voice on the other side of the door asked.

Marian gasped. "It is Mother. Robin, she cannot find you here!"

"No," Robin agreed, "she cannot. Just let me steal one last kiss." He leaned down and touched her lips gently with his own before climbing back through the still open window.

"When will I see you again?" Marian could not stop herself from asking the question.

"I will see you in Sherwood." He laughed when she could not stop the look of disappointment from crossing her face. "Do not worry, fair maid, time will pass swiftly enough."

"Marian du Luc, open the door this instant!"

"I have to go," Robin said. With a last wink at her he vanished back into the leaves.

"I am coming, Mother." Marian said. She walked swiftly to the bed and mussed the coverlet. "I was napping. You startled me." Three steps later she undid the bolt and pulled the door open.

"I thought I heard a man's laughter," Mother greeted, walking inside. Anna followed in her wake.

"Well, as you can plainly see, there is no one here," Marian gestured around her.

"And what is this?" Mother bent over, plucked the dogwood branch off the floor and held it up for Marian's inspection.

Marian blinked at her innocently. "Dogwood blossoms," she said.

"They are not in season," Mother said. "Where did you find them?"

"They were on the bed when I came up," Marian lied. "They must have fallen on the floor without my noticing."

Mother narrowed her eyes. "After you lay on the coverlet…" She waved one hand. "It does not matter. I came up to see if you were well. It appears you are. If you would like, I can send Anna back down to get you a tray."

Marian shook her head. "I think I am going to go back to bed. I did not sleep very well last night."

"As you like." Mother crossed over to the window and pulled it closed, latching it from the inside. "The nights are getting cooler and I do not want you catching anything. Be sure to keep the window shut."

"Yes, Mother." Marian agreed.

"Anna, you should not have left Marian alone," Mother admonished. "It was not proper, especially on such an important journey."

Tears welled up in the maid's eyes. "No, ma'am. It will not happen again."

"I told her she could go," Marian said. "All I was going to do was sleep, anyway."

"Even so," Mother said. "With the window left open, there was always the possibility of an outlaw finding his way inside."

Marian's eyes flew up to meet Mother's bland gaze. "You think someone could come in while I was sleeping?"

Mother's gaze flicked to the dogwood branch she still held. "The possibility always exists, though the probability is low." She handed the branch to Marian. "I shall see you in the morning. Tomorrow night we shall enjoy supper with Prince John, and I expect all of us to look our best."

"Supper at the castle!" Anna barely waited until the door shut behind Mother before she started chattering. "Imagine! Takin' a meal with the prince!"

"I am very tired, Anna." Marian cut her off. "Could you please help me into my night dress?"

"Oh. Of course, ma'am." Subdued, Anna helped Marian out of the lime green gown and into a long cotton shift.

"Good night." Marian crawled into bed, not waiting for Anna to blow out the two flickering candles on the end table. The double bed creaked slightly when the other girl slid under the coverlet, but Marian was already sliding into sleep.

Breakfast was an array of what Mother referred to as 'peasant fare', but Marian loved it. A thick, vegetable soup served with a slab of crusty bread and a large mug of still warm milk was placed in front of her as soon as she sat down.

The sheriff, seated across from Marian, grimaced. "I cannot wait," he said, "for supper tonight. Lady Marian, have you ever eaten larks tongues soaked in honey mead?"

Marian shook her head, grateful for the swallow of soup she had just taken, which prevented her from having to answer the question.

"I never cared for that dish," Mother dipped her bread into her soup. "It always reminded me of maggots swimming in sauce."

Laughter bubbled up in Marian's throat at Mother's description. Before it could escape her lips, she forced it back and began coughing.

"Mari, are you all right?" Father patted her on the back.

"I—yes." Marian coughed again.

The sheriff pushed his chair back from the table. "Larks tongues are a rare delicacy," he said. "I am sorry, Lady Beatrix, that your palate is no longer refined enough to enjoy them." He bowed abruptly. "Enjoy the rest of the meal. I shall leave six men here to escort you the rest of the way to Nottingham." Before anyone could respond, he stalked out the inn door, slamming it shut behind him.

"That was interesting," Mother said, dipping her bread into her soup again.

"Yes, it was," Father retorted.

Mother pushed her soup bowl away. "Are you quite ready, Mari?"

Marian pushed her own bowl away as well, having just finished her own soup. "Yes, Mother."

"Anna has already taken care of your sundries," Mother continued. She turned to Father. "What about the chest?"

Father nodded. "The chest is under our seat."

The wave of relief crossing Mother's face did not escape Marian's notice.

"What is so important about that chest?" She asked.

"Never mind," Mother said. "It is nothing for you to concern yourself with."

"You keep telling me that," Marian complained. She scooted her chair backwards and rose.

"Because it is the truth," Mother snapped. "Leave it alone, Marian."

Father held up one hand. "Beatrix, Marian, we are all under a tremendous amount of pressure. Let us just get to Nottingham, do what the prince wishes of us, then we can return home and sort everything else out."

Marian clenched her jaw, and then forced herself to relax it. Father was right. Nothing would be gained by pushing Mother for answers she was not willing to give. She placidly followed Mother and Father out to the waiting carriage, stepped inside and seated herself next to Anna.

"Just think!" Anna squealed in delight when the carriage lurched forward, "by tonight you will be supping with Prince John!"

Marian could hardly think of something *less* exciting, unless it was being seated next to the sheriff for said meal.

Mother glowered at the small maid. "I hardly think we shall be seated at Prince John's table," she said. "We have been summoned; we are not the prince's personal guests."

Anna glanced at Marian, who shrugged.

"Stop shrugging your shoulders, Marian." Mother instructed. "It is hardly ladylike, and wholly inappropriate for court."

Father smiled slightly. "Yes," he said, "we certainly would not want an unladylike child, Beatrix."

Mother glared at Father, but Marian was positive she could see a glimmer of laughter in her eyes.

"Watch the scenery, Mari," Father said. "The forest can be very enlightening if you know exactly what to watch for."

Marian sighed. As far as she could see, it was endless oaks in an endless sea of green and watching it roll by was not preferable to strolling the leaf strewn paths and smelling the almost damp scent of moldering undergrowth.

"Stop the carriage at once!" A strange voice cried out.

Anna screamed. "It is outlaws, ma'am! We will all be killed!"

"Hush," Father's normally gentle voice was threaded through with a core of steel Marian had never heard before. "Screaming will not help."

Mother hushed them with one upraised hand. Outside, Marian could hear voices raised in anger.

Chapter Nine:

A man's deep voice rang out clearly. "I do not recognize your authority. If you are the Sheriff of Nottingham's men, you must show me proof before you can pass."

"You must be new to your post," a deeper, more dangerous, voice growled back. "Stand down. We are on Prince John's business."

"You first," the first voice said flatly.

The unmistakable sound of hoof beats rang out, and then a familiar voice spoke. "What is going on here? Why are my men being detained?"

Marian heard a sword rasp as it was withdrawn.

"We have strict orders to let no one pass without proper authority," the first voice declared. "Prince John is sure there is a spy within the castle grounds. No-one is allowed to go further without permission."

"I am Prince John's oldest friend, and his sheriff, you dolt! I personally guarantee no-one here harbors any ill intent towards the prince or his rule!" The sheriff was nearly incoherent in his rage.

"And who are you carrying toward the castle?" The first man asked.

Mother stood up. "This is ridiculous," she stated. "Alan, let me by."

"Bea, this really is not—" Father started, but Mother pushed past him and opened the carriage door.

"Why is this carriage stopped?" An imperious voice Marian remembered hearing before, with Robin, demanded.

"Prince John's orders, milady," the first voice said.

"The prince is an idiot. I know who rides in that carriage. I will take full responsibility for anything she or her party may do."

Mother stepped backward, feeling with one hand before she sank back down to her seat. "It cannot be," she murmured. "I thought she died..."

"Beatrix, what is it?" Father asked worriedly. "You look pale."

A frown crossed Mother's face. "It is Lady Nyneve," she said. "Nottingham's historian. But she cannot still be alive...she would be over one hundred by now!"

Marian frowned. "And how does she know Ro..." she cut herself off at Mother's curious glance.

"Know who, Marian?" Mother asked.

Before Marian could think up a lie, the sheriff poked his head inside the still open door. "Is everything all right?"

Father nodded tersely. "My wife and daughter are tired," he said. "When can we continue on?"

Marian noticed the naked blade in the sheriff's hand at the same time Mother did.

"Sheriff, is a sword really necessary to get us past this patrol?" Mother said.

The sheriff slid the sword home. "It is my sworn duty to see you safely to the castle," he smiled. "If that means baring my blade, so be it."

"You are an idiot, too," Nyneve stuck her head in the window next to Marian. "Hello, child. Curious we should meet again in this fashion. Stop gaping, Beatrix. Yes, it is me. Yes, I am alive." She smiled at Alan, a hint of rose creeping up into her withered cheeks. "And the famous Alan a Dale. I have heard many a tale about your ballads. I hope you shall grace us with one at the castle. Provided, of course, you can actually *get* there." Nyneve glared at the sheriff until he eased the door closed. "I will see you upon your arrival."

"She scares me," Anna whispered as the carriage began to lurch forward once more. "And she says you know her?"

Marian squirmed under Father's glare and Mother's questioning look. "I do not exactly *know* her," she said. "I met her in the forest. Briefly."

"How interesting that you met her, yet never said a word," Mother mused. "I find that terribly enlightening."

"It did not mean anything," Marian mumbled.

"Obviously it did, or she would not recall it."

"When did you meet her?" Father asked. "Was it recently?"

Marian smiled gratefully. Finally, there was an answer she could give without directly lying. "I met her two days ago, but we barely spoke."

"She always did prefer the forest to the castle," Mother said, almost under her breath. "What were you doing that caught her attention?"

Marian bit her lip. "I was – practicing my fencing."

"Ah, yes, that *would* bring you to her notice," Father said.

"But why?" Marian asked.

"The sword you carry is ancient," he said. "It stands to reason that a historian of all things English would be curious about it."

"I shall have to speak with her upon our arrival," Mother decided. "I have many questions I wish to ask her."

"She appears nice enough," Father said. "I would love to speak with her myself. I am sure she can tell me things about Nottingham even I do not know."

"Did you bring my sword?" Marian asked suddenly.

Mother laughed. "Of course not! It is one thing to wear it about town, but never at court. No decent woman would ever be seen carrying a blade!"

Marian opened her mouth to respond, but just then Anna gasped.

"Look, ma'am! Outside! It is the castle!"

Marian looked and saw Nottingham Castle before them, sprawled out across the landscape like a patchwork quilt she had once seen in a shop's window; beautifully constructed, but made of the dullest cloth imaginable.

"It is—ugly," Marian blurted, drawing her head back inside the carriage.

"It is a fortress, Marian," Mother said. "It was not built to be attractive."

Marian was disappointed. The castle looked lifeless despite the guards patrolling the tall gray stone wall that extended from either side of the portcullis and vanished past where her eyes could easily see. As their carriage pulled through the gate, Marian craned her head out the window once more, only she was pulled backward by Mother's firm grip.

"What do you think you are doing? You look like a country bumpkin who's never seen a castle before! Sit back before someone sees you."

Marian bounced once on the seat, earning a glare from Mother. "But it is what I am," she protested. "What is wrong with that?"

"You cannot stick your head out the window like a goose. Keep your head inside, and look as we pass by, like this."

Marian watched as Mother leaned slightly forward, and turned her head toward her window. "Remember, Marian, ladies do not gawk."

Marian rested her chin on her hand and stared moodily out at the passing wall. The most interesting thing she saw was twelve guards, standing stiffly at attention, their gaze never wavering from the opposite wall.

As they reached the doors to the inner courtyard, the carriage halted, the horses snorting and stamping their feet.

"Anna, go assist the footmen with Marian's things." Mother commanded.

The maid agreed, her naturally wide brown eyes even wider.

"I will go find the sheriff," Father said. "Presumably, he will know which rooms are ours and can direct the footmen."

"Thank you, Alan. You are correct," Mother said. "Marian, follow me."

Marian obeyed instantly. However ugly the castle was on the outside, she was eager to see what waited within its walls.

"Lady Marian, Lady Beatrix, I am so pleased you arrived so swiftly." The sheriff appeared at Marian's elbow as soon as she stepped down from the carriage. "What do you think of the castle so far?"

She lowered her eyes but answered his question honestly. "It does not look like I expected it to."

The sheriff laughed; a bellowing sound. Nearby guards glanced at them before continuing their duties. "The inside is vastly different.

Prince John has ensured none of his guests will suffer any discomfort in *his* care. Let me show you." He tightened his grip on her elbow.

"Sheriff, we would prefer to be shown our quarters," Mother said, "though your attentiveness to our comfort has not gone unnoticed." She glanced down at the sheriff's grip on Marian. "Marian, dear, your hand is rather dirty. I think a washing is in order before you soil the good sheriff's shirt, do not you?"

The sheriff grimaced and released Marian. "May I have the pleasure of escorting you both indoors?" He offered his arm to Mother instead, who took it immediately.

"Of course. Come along, Marian."

"As I was saying," the sheriff motioned and two guards pulled the enormous wooden doors leading to the main hall open, "Prince John has spared no expense in his treatment of his loyal subjects."

There *was* comfort. Across from Marian, a huge fire blazed in a fireplace that would have easily accommodated four men standing side by side and three deep. Tapestries hung on every wall, clashing in swirls of color that made her head ache. Everywhere she looked there were men and women, each more elaborately gowned, bedecked and jeweled than herself. Marian's hand inadvertently rose to the back of her neck and the hasty knot she had tied her hair into.

"Do not fret, Marian," even Mother's voice was welcome amid all the chatter. "It is not seemly. Sheriff, would you see what has become of my husband? He left us outside saying he would search for you. I presume you did not see him?"

The man shook his head. "No, but I can send someone to search." He snapped his fingers and a small page came running. "Find Alan a Dale. He just arrived and will be carrying a lute. He will also be inquiring about me."

The little boy nodded, looking solemn and far older than his years, which Marian guessed was about seven. "Alan a Dale, who carries a lute." He scampered off.

"A trainee," the sheriff said. "I am sorry you had to see such manners." He smiled at Marian. "Do not let his lack of discipline form your opinions of how the castle runs. Prince John is very strict, but fair."

"Training has to start somewhere," Marian said. "I saw nothing wrong with his manners."

"We are grateful for your insights," Mother interrupted. "It has been a long time since I have visited court, and I can see how things have changed with King Richard's departure."

"Yes, the king was a good man," the sheriff looked almost sick at mention of him. "But he is fighting a Holy Crusade, and left his kingdom in very capable hands."

Mother arched one eyebrow as she took in the hordes of people, the raucous laughter and the dancing that even now was taking place. "Yes, I can see that. Prince John has done an admirable job of following in his brother's footsteps and taking care of his kingdom."

Chapter Ten:

The sheriff narrowed his eyes. "Are you by chance a sympathizer of Hood, Lady Beatrix?"

Mother stiffened. "How dare you question my loyalty to the crown! The du Luc family has always been above reproach." She removed her hand from the sheriff's arm. "Marian, I think we would be best served to search for your father ourselves. Please excuse us, Sheriff. It is a bit close in here. I need some fresh air."

The sheriff's mouth opened, and then closed. He bowed jerkily. "Please accept my apologies. I did not mean to insult you or your family name."

"Ah, there you are, Sheriff." Father strolled up. "Your page found me." He put an arm around Mother. "Is everything all right, Beatrix?"

Mother nodded. "What kept you?"

"One of the horses turned up lame. But it has been taken care of."

Marian paled. "It—it was not killed, was it?"

"Of course not," Father reassured her. "I doubt even Prince John could afford to waste such a valuable commodity."

"The prince does not believe in wasting anything valuable," the sheriff agreed. "And neither do I," he continued with a sideways glance at Marian.

She hid a shudder at the look in his eyes. His gaze held all the warmth of a cold, foggy day.

"Sheriff," Mother cut into the conversation. "Do get someone to show us to our rooms. I am tired and want to rest before supper."

"I can do that," the sheriff protested. "There's no need to bother the servants."

"They are servants," Mother said with a sniff. "I do not see how it would be a bother for them to do their job."

The sheriff bowed. "But you are Prince John's special guests. He would be most displeased if I did not make sure the accommodations were to your satisfaction." He led the way through the Great Hall, dodging servants with ease.

Marian followed dutifully after them, grateful the sheriff was not insisting she walk at his side. Her skin crawled whenever he looked at her; as though she were nothing more than a prettily packaged life sized doll.

The comparatively silent stone hallway bustled with household servants, each quietly going about their respective business. At one point, Marian was forced back against the stone wall as servants clad in matching tunics and leggings of purple and silver marched past her, steam rising from the platters they held high above their heads.

"It smells delicious." Marian's mouth began to water. She raised herself onto her toes, peeking at the platters as they went by. Peacocks in wine, tail feathers fanned out across the wooden platter in resplendent glory; a whole roasted boar, apple tucked neatly into its mouth; platters upon platters of cheese, eggs, and more pastries than Marian had ever seen.

"I do not see any larks' tongues," the sheriff said, his voice thick with disapproval. "They should always be served when the prince is in attendance."

"Does Prince John like them?" Marian asked.

"Of course," the sheriff said, "or they would not be placed at his table. I do hope you will do me the courtesy of trying one over supper. They truly are a rare delicacy, and melt in the mouth."

Marian could not imagine anything more foul. "I am sure the larks see things rather differently," she said.

"Marian du Luc, apologize at once!" Mother scolded.

Father attempted to look stern, but it was ruined by the tears of laughter which welled up in his eyes.

Marian glanced at the ground. "I do apologize," she murmured. "I should not have said it."

"You might wish to guard that tongue closer," the sheriff returned. "The prince does not see the humor in a sharp witted woman."

"Sheriff, I think it wise if you guard your own tongue around my daughter," Father bit out. "Your veiled threats are insulting and will not be tolerated."

The other man bowed immediately, but not before Marian saw the anger in his eyes. "I did not mean any offense. Please accept my humble apologies."

Mother nodded once. "Will we have time to make ourselves respectable before supper? I would hate to see the prince while still dressed in the filth from the road."

"The prince would never wish you to look anything but your best." The sheriff's smile was oily and reminded Marian strongly of a charlatan who had once travelled through their town.

"Come, the hallway is clear enough for us to continue."

They wound their way through the castle halls and a staircase, stopping only when the sheriff paused before a set of double doors.

"These suites have been set aside for your personal use," he said. "Your chests have already been delivered." He turned to Marian. "I do hope you will see fit to join me at supper. I cannot imagine a greater pleasure than sharing a plate with you."

Mother immediately shook her head. "I am sorry to deny you, Sheriff, but I fear Marian's palate varies greatly from yours and I would not dream of denying you the comforts of your belly."

"Very well. The servants have already begun serving the lower tables. *Our* tables will not be served until Prince John arrives, so you have time to rest yourselves and change."

"Thank you, Sheriff." Father pulled open the doors and stood aside for Mother and Marian. "We shall see you downstairs, then."

"Yes, thank you for all your kindness," Mother said dismissively. Only once the doors were shut behind them did she sigh deeply. "What an odious man."

The sitting room was a riot of gold and green. Thick green velvet hangings trimmed in gold covered what Marian took at first glance to be stone walls. Upon closer inspection she realized they covered large, diamond shaped windows. She stared through the bubbled surface down at the distorted images of soldiers standing in the courtyard.

"Is the castle always so heavily fortified?" Marian asked curiously.

"It never was under King Richard's rule," Mother said.

"Prince John probably has extra guards because of what the sheriff told us about possible spies," Father said. "Marian, why not go and look at your rooms? They are very likely through that doorway." He pointed across the room.

"I—have my own rooms here?" Marian practically danced across the room, past two chairs and a low reclining couch also covered in thick green velvet. "Were your rooms like these, when you lived here?"

"I never lived here," Mother said. "I stayed in London."

"Then how do you know court has changed so much?" Marian paused at the doorway.

Mother shrugged delicately. "One court is very much like another," she said. "And Prince John always enjoyed his—baser—comforts more than Richard did."

"So you knew him, then?"

"I knew *of* him. I was raised at court, Marian. I was not a confidant of either Richard or John. Now stop pestering me and go look at your rooms."

Marian meandered through the doorway in the opposite wall separating the sitting room from the bedrooms. Off the larger room, whose opulence rivaled the room she had just left, was a smaller bedroom with a single wide bed. A rich emerald comforter was spread across it, large pillows piled high. Prince John had spared no expense to ensure his guests were well satisfied with their surroundings.

Marian sat on the bed. If this was how he was using his money—she blinked. Not his money. *Their* money. The heavy, unfair taxes her family and others like them paid were being used to keep Prince John and his court in luxury. And while the tax collectors were doing that, they were also lowering the morale of King Richard's people. By the time the king returned, his people would no longer care. That, she realized, was when the real war would begin. It was not overseas, fighting for Christianity. It would be here, in England, between two brothers, one the rightful king, the other nothing more than a fraud.

She felt sick. No wonder Robin did what he did. What other choice was there?

"Marian, I need you out here, please." Mother's voice broke through her musing. "We must dress for supper."

Marian rose. Choosing a gown would be far easier than thinking over the prince's plans for England.

"What would you rather wear?" Mother greeted her, holding up a concoction of crimson and gold. "Would you rather wear this or," she put the gown down and picked up another, "this?" The latter gown was deep emerald, edged at the hem and sleeves with silver thread that sparkled and glittered in the candlelight.

"The emerald," Marian said, glad Mother was giving her a choice at all.

"With your hair pinned up, you will look appropriate enough for the prince's table." Mother motioned to Anna. "Her hair must be up, but not completely," she directed as Marian took a seat at the small vanity. "I want curls hanging down on either side of her face, and this," she handed the maid a finger wide silver band, "threaded into the hair above her forehead."

Anna nodded; her hands already finger combing Marian's long hair. Before Marian realized it, her hair was pulled, pinned and prodded into shape.

"Lovely," Father said. "Now, if you ladies would excuse me, I will go practice my ballad elsewhere so you can dress." He smiled at Marian. "You look stunning. You will not want for dance partners."

Marian blushed.

"Goodness, Marian, if you blush every time someone compliments you, everyone will think you are nothing more than a poor relation," Mother scolded. "Tonight is for you to see and be seen. Make the best impression you can, but do not, under any circumstances, make a promise to anyone about anything without speaking to me first."

"Go, Alan, so we can get ready," Mother scolded with a smile. Father bowed extravagantly, and blew a kiss in their direction as he backed out the doors and pulled them shut.

"Now let us get you dressed properly." At Mother's instruction, Anna removed Marian's travelling gown and carefully lowered the emerald confection over her head.

Marian felt beautiful. The green silk caressed her skin as she spun in a circle.

"Anna, we will not need you tonight. You can get a plate from the kitchens."

"Yes, ma'am." The girl scurried past them and let herself out the doors.

"She will not be coming with us?" Marian asked. "Are you sure a lady's maid is not necessary?"

Mother shook her head. "Not for supper. Come, neither the meal nor the prince will wait on us, regardless of what the sheriff says."

They strolled out the doors, through the halls and back down stairs, where Marian could see servants pouring both into and out of the Great Hall.

Chapter Eleven:

Marian stabbed at the sliced eggs on the bread trencher she shared with Mother while Father chatted with the woman seated next to him. The meal was endless, servants filing past the trestle tables, placing platter after platter of food onto the already overburdened surface. She wished she could have escaped the whole affair. Her eyes flicked up from her trencher and met the gaze of an older gentleman at the next table. He smiled and she lowered her eyes.

"Marian, what is the matter with you? You should be eating." Mother said. "Are the eggs undercooked?"

"No, the eggs are fine." They were. Swimming in an unidentifiable sauce, but fine as far as she could tell. She eyed them as they sat on her trencher.

"You will insult our host if you refuse to eat," Mother said.

"Where *is* the prince?" Marian asked. "I thought the sheriff said he would be in attendance."

"Royalty never arrives on time," Mother sniffed. "You need to eat."

"I—I am not used to being stared at." Marian faltered under Mother's stern gaze.

Mother laughed. "Is that all?" She waved a hand to encompass the entire hall. "I see no one staring at you."

"It has only been two people," Marian confessed. "That man over there, with the red hair and freckles, and a woman at our table, seated at the end. They do not stare at me all the time, just enough to make me uncomfortable."

Mother shrugged. It was a delicate gesture that barely rippled the shoulders of her ivory silk gown. "I would not concern myself with it. Concentrate on your meal. You will need to eat something before the dancing officially begins."

Marian's eyes widened. "Dancing?"

Mother sighed. "You know how to dance. And you *will* dance." Her voice was firm.

Marian turned toward Father, but he was no longer there. She looked around and saw him walking in between the tables, laughing and looking perfectly at home.

She went back to stabbing the innocent eggs.

"Lady Marian, is the food not to your liking?"

Marian looked up into the sheriff's concerned eyes. "Everything is fine, thank you."

"Then why are you not eating?"

To her dismay, he slid onto the bench next to her, forcing the nobleman on her left to shift over.

"The dancing is about to begin," the sheriff continued. "Are you sure I cannot tempt you with something?"

Marian shook her head. "I will try and eat something later. I am too nervous to eat now."

"Then may I have the honor of the first dance?"

Marian forced a smile onto her face and nodded.

"I would be pleased to dance with you," she lied.

"Lady Marian?" The soft voice caught her attention and she met the widely spaced eyes of the older gentleman who had been staring at her throughout supper.

She smiled as the sheriff glowered. "Yes?"

"Would you honor me with this dance?"

"She is mine," the sheriff stated.

Marian looked at Mother for help, but none was forthcoming. The older woman sat with her back to Marian. Marian's jaw clenched before she answered. "I am afraid the first dance has already been promised, but the following ones are unspoken for."

The sheriff's eyes narrowed, but his voice was honeyed. "Lady Marian, he is here at the sufferance of Prince John. There is no need to indulge his request."

The older man's face flushed.

Marian stiffened. "And I am here solely due to my mother's ties to the crown, Sheriff. He and I are here for the same reasons."

"Hardly the same reasons, Lady Marian. You are royalty. He is—nothing." The sheriff waved his hand in a dismissing gesture.

"Sheriff," Marian's voice was cold. "I promised you the first dance. Do not presume more than I have offered."

Without warning, the sheriff smiled. "I would never presume with you, Lady Marian. Very well. If you choose to dance with this—this person, I will not stand in your way."

Marian nodded at him, not trusting herself to speak. The first piping notes of a lute rose high into the air.

"I see your father decided to play for us even though the prince is not here."

"He has a ballad he wished to perform for the historian," Marian said. "But this is not the piece. He must intend this piece to lead into the next one."

"Ah, yes, the Lady Nyneve. She is—an interesting woman," the sheriff said. He glared at the man. "The first dance is mine."

Marian smiled at the flustered gentleman. "After Father sings," she promised. She took the sheriff's offered hand, allowing him to draw her onto the dance floor.

"Tell me, Sheriff, are the rumors about Prince John true?"

"What rumors are you referring to, Lady Marian?" He spun her around.

When she was once more in his arms, she answered. "As you know, I live within walking distance of Sherwood Forest. There are rumors that Prince John has placed a price on every man's head that makes the forest his home."

"If you are referring to the outlaws, then those rumors are, indeed, fact." His hand tightened on hers until she nearly cried out.

She pulled her hand away and rubbed at it, glaring at him while couples swirled around them.

"Lady Marian, I apologize." He reached for her hand again and she let him take it. "I do not know what came over me. There are certain people who have started rumors in the hopes of destroying Prince John's rule. While the prince certainly does not wish to see anyone within his kingdom hung, he feels it is best for England if all outlaws are brought to a swift and immediate justice."

"But they have done nothing wrong," Marian found herself protesting.

"Nothing wrong?" The sheriff frowned. "Lady Marian, I do not know who you have been listening to, but those men are wanted criminals by the throne. They are hardly the innocents you apparently believe they are." His eyes narrowed as the music faded. "Unless... Lady Marian, are you a sympathizer of outlaws?"

"Of course not!" Marian snatched her hands away. "Thank you for the dance, sheriff, but I am tired and wish to listen to my father perform."

"Naturally. I am glad you graced me with your presence. I do hope I can claim another dance before this evening ends." He bowed, turned on his heel abruptly and walked away.

"Lady Marian?"

She blinked, her gaze focusing on the skinny, fire-haired man the Sheriff had berated.

His prominent Adam's apple bobbed as he swallowed. "You promised me a dance?"

Marian nodded.

"I am Lord Aelfred Phismore the Third."

She smiled at him. "And you apparently already know who I am."

"The whole c—court is whispering your name." He grinned at her shocked look. "You are the daughter of Lady Beatrix du Luc herself."

Marian barely heard Father begin to sing, his baritone voice rising high above the drawn out notes of his lute.

"My mother? How does everyone know of me through my mother?"

Lord Aelfred blinked. "You do not know?"

"Know what?" Marian asked. "What am I supposed to know that everyone else does?

"Maybe we should go outside."

Marian shook her head. "I cannot, Lord Aelfred, my maid did not accompany me to supper and I have no one else to chaperone us."

"I would never suggest any impropriety," he said.

"I was not saying you would." Marian was quick to reassure him. "But my mother would kill me if she knew I was even *considering* such a thing."

Lord Aelfred leaned in close, and lowered his voice. "Then you already know what she is," he whispered.

"What?!" Marian pulled back. "Are you calling her a murderer??"

The gentleman looked utterly shocked. "A murderer? Of c— course not!" He met her puzzled expression. "You really have no idea what I am t—talking about, do you?"

"No, I do not. And I certainly do not appreciate the innuendo about my mother."

"I—never mind. I should not have said anything. Would you c— care for some mead? You look flushed." Without waiting for an answer, the nonplussed Lord Aelfred vanished into the crowd.

Chapter Twelve:

Marian watched the dancers swirl around her while she waited for Lord Aelfred's return. It was obvious he knew something about Mother, and she was determined to learn exactly what that was.

"Here is your c—cup." A goblet was thrust into her hands.

"Thank you, Lord Aelfred," Marian said. She sipped the golden liquid and nearly choked at the first swallow. "It really is sweet, isn't it?"

He laughed. "Yes, if you are not used to it. And please c—call me Aelfred."

Marian smiled. In spite of what he had not told her about Mother, she liked him. He was sincere and very unlike the sheriff. "Only if you will do me the same courtesy, and call me Marian. I am not used to having 'Lady' attached to my name."

"How long will you be at c—court?" Aelfred asked.

"We shall be here as long as Prince John decrees, I imagine."

"Prince John," Aelfred repeated.

Marian blinked. "Yes, that is what I said."

"No, look, it is Prince John!" Aelfred bowed low, head bent.

Marian gasped, her eyes automatically searching the hall. The prince waded through the dancers, who parted before him like water around a large stone, until he reached Marian.

"Lady Marian du Luc, we are so glad you could join us." The tall, thin man, head slightly too large for the shoulders it sat on, gazed down at her.

She stifled the urge to giggle at the sight, instead sweeping into a low curtsey. "Your Highness."

"And you, Lord Aelfred. Have you been keeping Lady Marian company all evening?"

Aelfred flushed. "Only this one dance, Highness."

Prince John nodded. "Walk with us, Lady Marian." He took Marian's hand and drew her towards the huge fireplace. "As a child, I was interested in all aspects of history, especially as it related to the throne." His hand brushed a curl away from her face, fingers lingering against her cheek. "I am curious, Lady Marian, about your ancestors."

Marian blinked. "I am not sure I understand what you're asking, Highness."

The prince smiled. "You are such an innocent," he murmured. "Allow me to be blunt, then. I am most curious about your knowledge of Excalibur."

"What is that?" Marian asked.

Before the prince could reply, Mother hurried up to where they stood. "Highness, it is good to see you again! My husband and I were so pleased to receive your summons."

"Lady Beatrix, you finally grace us with your presence." Prince John turned to Mother. "You have been greatly missed."

"You are too kind, Highness. Has my daughter been keeping you good company?"

"She is charming," Prince John said. "We were just speaking of certain aspects of your history."

Mother laughed. "Should you wish to know anything about our family, Highness, all you need to do is ask. I would be more than pleased to answer any of your questions."

"I will admit," Prince John said, "an interest in a certain blade rumored to be within your family."

"The only blade we have is an old, nearly worthless one," Mother said. "It would be of no interest to you, Highness."

The prince gazed at Mother for a long, silent moment. "The blade I speak of can be nowhere else," he murmured before addressing Mother directly. "Then where, Lady Beatrix, is Excalibur?"

Marian stared at Mother. "What is Excalibur?"

"Excalibur is a legend, nothing more." Mother said.

"It is the most famous sword in history," Prince John explained. "It was pulled from a stone by King Arthur and protected him from all serious harm during his reign. I have it on good authority it can now be found somewhere in England."

Mother's laugh was shaky. "Did your source not tell you it was returned to the Lady of the Lake upon King Arthur's death? I thought that was common knowledge."

"I would not be doing my duty as—regent—of the throne if I refused to investigate such information thoroughly, common knowledge or not."

A small frown crossed Prince John's forehead as a young page hurried across the floor toward him.

"Highness." The page waited for the prince's nod. "The sheriff wishes a word with you."

"What was important enough to interrupt me?"

The little boy gulped. "He said it was about the problem in the forest."

"Ah," the prince nodded. "I see." He turned back toward Marian. "Lady Marian, Lady Beatrix, I fear other duties claim my attention. I do hope we have the chance to converse again. It has proven very— enlightening." He smiled tightly before walking away.

"Why would Prince John be interested in an old sword?" Marian asked Mother.

"Excalibur was very powerful during the time of King Arthur, Marian. But why John thinks it resides in England, I have no idea. It vanished into history, just like The Lady of the Lake and Camelot itself."

"Why would he believe we have it?"

Mother sighed. "Lancelot du Luc was The Lady of the Lake's son. Marian, I understand that Camelot is in our distant past, but what happened there was fact, not fiction. You need to pay more attention to your history lessons." She raised one hand to stop Marian's next question. "Enough. This is not the time to speak of such matters. Come sit with me. The acrobats are about to begin."

Marian raised a hand to her mouth and yawned. "Do you think I can just go up to our rooms?"

Mother shook her head. "No, it would be unbearably rude to our host to leave in the midst of his planned entertainments."

Marian sighed.

"Marian du Luc, what is wrong with you?" Mother admonished. "It is your first night at court and you seem bored with it all."

"I am not bored," Marian protested. "I did not sleep well before we left. I am simply tired."

Mother bit her lip, then nodded. "Very well then, you can go up. I will make your excuses to Prince John, should he ask about you."

"Thank you, Mother." Marian glanced once at the acrobats already performing before she slipped out into the relatively quiet hallway.

"*She does not understand,*" a young voice whispered.

"*Should we tell her the truth?*" Boyish laughter followed the question.

"*We are not allowed to, remember?*"

Marian glanced around her. The only people in the hall were servants, carrying empty platters from the Great Hall.

There was another burst of laughter.

"Did you hear that?" Marian stopped a passing servant with a hand on his arm.

He nodded. "It is the ghosts, milady. They always babble more when the prince is in residence."

"What ghosts?"

"You do not know, milady? This place is haunted." He lowered his voice. "It is a fact that the boys were murdered, right here in the castle."

"*Yes,*" a young voice agreed. "*Murdered. Taken from our beds…*"

The servant pulled away from Marian. "Excuse me, milady. I have already said more than I should about it."

"*Hidden secrets,*" multiple voices whispered. "*More than she knows.*" There was another burst of high pitched laughter.

"Be careful," the servant threw the warning over his shoulder. "Be sure to stay away from the battlements. The boys seem to like you, but their sense of humor can be deadly."

The ghosts laughed again but this time the laughter seemed sinister. The sound sent a shiver down Marian's spine.

"*You scared her.*" An older boy's voice stated. "*You shall have to answer to them. They want her to stay.*"

There was no response. Marian gathered her skirts in one hand and ran down the hall and up the stairs to her suite of rooms. Only once she was inside, with the doors shut firmly behind her, did she lean back against them and close her eyes.

"Will was right," she whispered incredulously. "They actually exist."

There was only one place she could think of to go next, and it was not to her bedchamber. Opening the doors once more, she slipped out and down the halls toward the chapel.

Chapter Thirteen:

Two robed figures knelt in front of the large wooden cross. Marian bowed her head respectfully and walked to the front of the chapel. She knelt, closing her eyes.

"Help me, Lord," she whispered.

"May I be of some service?"

Marian met the gaze of the friar next to her, a slight smile on his wrinkled face. She shook her head. "No, Friar. I could not sleep, so I thought I would come here to pray."

"I can pray with you, my lady. What troubles you?"

Marian bit the corner of her lip. "I am new to the castle," she said. "It is a bit overwhelming."

"Father, it is late," the second friar said. "Go to bed. I will take your place in prayer."

Marian had to look up to meet the second friar's startlingly green eyes. He smiled, his teeth white in his deeply tanned face.

"Thank you, my son." The elder man got slowly to his feet, bones creaking loudly in the quiet. "May He bless you, child." He made the sign of the cross in the air before Marian, shuffled down the aisle and out the chapel door.

"There was only one family summoned to the castle recently," the remaining friar said. "You would be the Lady Marian du Luc, correct?"

"I—yes. How did you know?"

The friar rose to his feet. "My name is Friar Tuck. I believe we have a mutual friend outside these walls."

"How do I know you are who you say you are?" Marian asked suspiciously.

"You are questioning whether I am a friar?" The man asked.

"You do not look like a man of the cloth." She stared at him, arms crossed. He was tall, with well muscled forearms. He looked everything like a swordsman and nothing like she expected a friar to look.

"Is that all?" Tuck laughed. "I was not born a friar, Lady Marian." He knelt in front of her, his hands resting on his knees. "I will not bore you with an account of my misdeeds, or what path led me to this one. Suffice to say, I *am* a friar, albeit one whose questionable temper made my superior give me this," he paused for a moment before continuing, "perfectly lovely assignment."

"That does not explain your belief of a mutual friend."

Tuck shook his head. "He never told me you were so suspicious. Very well, what 'proof' would you accept of my claim?"

"Tell me something only our mutual friend would know."

"When he sent me word of your impending arrival, he also told me of your meeting with Nottingham's historian and of the sword fight you lost."

"I did not lose," Marian snapped. "She distracted me!"

The friar laughed. "So…proof enough for you, then?"

Marian nodded. There was no way Tuck would know of the incident, save from Robin's men. It was proof she could accept.

"Now that you believe I am who I claim to be, is there something specific I can help you with?" Tuck asked.

Marian sighed. "It is everything. Prince John believes I know the whereabouts of a sword I never believed existed, my mother is hiding something, and there are ghosts in the castle. I feel like I do not fit in here."

Tuck smiled and seated himself next to her. "You do not fit in," he said bluntly. "You are royalty that is not royal. That is a rarity, especially here." He shook his head. "As a man of the cloth, I cannot reveal anything I have been told in confidence, even if it is pertinent to you and yours. It would violate everything I believe in. However," he placed one hand over Marian's. "I think you would find great comfort in the gardens tomorrow, should you choose to explore them. The maze is especially nice this time of year. You can see many different kinds of birds if you look hard enough."

She peered at him. "Are you saying..."

"I am saying you should go see the gardens." Tuck repeated. "Certain birds tend to appear unexpectedly." He glanced up at the stained glass windows. "It will be light soon. You should return to your rooms."

"Thank you, Friar." She returned to her rooms through halls already full of servants rubbing at their eyes as they began their daily chores. It was nearly dawn.

"Marian, have you been gone all night?" Mother's voice greeted her when Marian opened the doors to their suite. "You had us worried *sick*."

"Yes, Marian, we are waiting for an explanation." Father crossed sinewy arms over his chest.

"I—I did not think you would miss me," Marian stuttered. "I could not sleep, so I went to the chapel to pray."

"And you did not think to wake Anna and take her with you?" Mother shook her head. "Marian du Luc, what were you thinking?"

Marian lowered her eyes to the ground. "I was thinking I did not need her," she mumbled at her feet.

"She is to go wherever you go, Marian," Father said.

"You cannot behave as you did at home." Mother tugged the belt on her dressing gown, tightening it. "Your behavior is unacceptable."

"Unacceptable to you, you mean." Marian raised her eyes to meet Mother's steady hazel gaze.

"It is unacceptable to everyone, Marian," Father said sharply. "You owe your mother an apology."

"Am I allowed to go the chapel at all?"

"Of course you are," Mother said. "As long as you and Anna go there together."

Realizing Mother could ban her from any small freedoms, Marian bowed to the inevitable. "I am sorry, Mother. I should not have left without Anna."

Mother stared at her for a long moment before she spoke. "Go to bed, Marian. You look tired. Once you are rested, come to the gardens. They are lovely this time of year and you should not miss them."

"Do not," Father instructed, "forget to bring Anna with you. She is in the kitchens."

Marian nodded sleepily, yawning behind her hand as she walked across the room to her suite.

Chapter Fourteen:

Later that afternoon, Marian stared at the gardens in abundant summertime bloom, lords and ladies already walking among the perfectly shaped hedges.

They looked glorious, but crowded with people. Anna hovered at her elbow, her eyes wide. "I never thought I would see castle gardens," she said. "They are beautiful."

Marian agreed. She just wished she could wander through them without a maid at her elbow. It was apparent she was not the only young woman who felt that way, either. Maids scurried after their mistresses, who hurried along without regard for their young chaperones. She had two choices. See the gardens with Anna, or spend the day sitting on a bench. Taking a deep breath, she let it out slowly and spoke. "Let us go see the maze garden."

A low stone wall, honeysuckle draped over it like a blanket, edged the footpath leading to the garden maze. Blackbirds and small gray sparrows flitted among the cherry trees and rose bushes, dislodging petals of pink, white and blue, sending them cascading to the ground. Marian gazed around in delight. Firethorn bushes lined both sides of the footpath, far enough back from the wall to prevent accidental injuries. Bees and butterflies flew from flower to flower, collecting pollen.

"I have never seen anything like this," Anna said, her voice low. "Why are so few people here, though?"

Marian glanced around. The further they walked from the castle and the formal gardens, the less people there were. Was the maze that uninteresting? She could see the start of it up ahead, the yews rising into the air beyond the wide stone archway.

"I—I do not think I can go in there," Anna stared through the stone arch. "Those trees are awfully high."

Marian turned to stare at her maid. "You live on the edge of Sherwood," she said. "Surely you are not scared of a few trees."

Anna shook her head. "It is not the trees that scare me. But look how close together they are."

It was lovely. True, the yews looked so close together she would have to walk sideways in some places, but that hardly bothered Marian. She looked at Anna again. The girl was almost shivering in fear, arms hugged close to her chest.

"I know you are supposed to go with me," Marian began slowly.

Tears formed in the maid's eyes. "I am sorry, Lady Marian, but I cannot. I just cannot. The trees, they are too...big."

"They are not any larger than the trees in Sherwood," Marian said.

"They look huge," Anna shook her head. "Please do not make me go in there."

"It will be all right, Anna. I shall explain it to Mother. Go back to the gardens and wait for me there I should not be too long."

"Thank you." The young girl turned away from the stone arch and almost ran back toward the castle.

Marian released a sigh. Without a backward glance, she walked through the arch and entered the narrow corridor of yew trees.

The trees closed around Marian. It was comforting and reminded her of home. She stepped deeper into the maze, the sleeves of her blue linen gown catching on the closeness of the yew trees limbs. Laughter echoed through the maze, though she could not tell where it came from. The air was cool, the heavy scent of honeysuckle blanketing the maze. The path ahead of her split, curving both left and right. She was sure the left-hand path would lead to the center of the maze eventually. Smiling to herself, she walked around the right hand curve instead.

"I half expected you to take the other path," the young man in front of her said, seeming to appear out of nowhere.

Marian swallowed her scream. "Robin, you nearly scared me to death!"

He lifted his head so she could see him under the hood of the friar's robe he wore. "Sorry," he said unrepentantly.

"What on earth are you doing here? And why are you dressed like that?"

"I came to see you, of course."

She blushed at the thought. "If Prince John catches you—"

He finished her sentence. "I will spend my better years in his dungeon, if he does not outright kill me for my crimes."

"What if someone sees us together?" Her heart leapt at the thought.

"The parapets are empty, see?" He pointed up and over the yew trees.

No-one was standing at the castle walls, looking down. "Can they really see into the maze from there?"

Robin nodded. He took her hand in his. "Come on, the path widens a bit further in."

Marian followed him through the curves and twists until they reached a dead-end covered in honeysuckle. "How do you know so much about the maze?"

"King Richard had the maze planted when he was made heir apparent to the throne." Robin turned to frown at her. "I am surprised you do not know this. Your town's Master Carpenter worked on the bridges."

"What bridges?"

Robin brushed aside the clinging vine to reveal a dark passageway. "The bridges in the garden, of course. King Richard wanted to make sure his court could find their way out of the maze without too much trouble. He had the Master Carpenter build bridges so people in the maze could see where they were."

"What was the passageway for?" Marian asked.

Robin shrugged. "I have no idea, but it leads straight into Sherwood Forest."

She peered into the inky corridor. "Is this how you got here?"

"Yes," Robin said. "Now step inside and be careful. There are three steps in front of you."

Marian stepped into the passageway and down, the sharp scent of dirt tickling her nose. Darkness closed around her as Robin let the honeysuckle vine fall back into place.

She felt him take her hands in his. "I have a favor to ask of you, Marian, but it is not without risk."

She could not control the excitement that colored her words. "What is it?"

"One of my men has learned of a rumor that the sheriff is planning to steal the throne from under Prince John."

"But—it is not Prince John's throne," Marian said.

"No, it is not. But neither John nor the sheriff care about such trivialities."

She could barely see the shape of his face in the dim light. "Are you telling me Prince John wants King Richard's throne?"

He nodded. "I think so, but my source in the castle has certain restrictions which limit his usefulness. That is where I need your help."

"I do not know what help I can be, but I am willing to try."

"I need you to learn everything you can about the prince's plans," Robin said earnestly.

Marian hesitated. "You…want me to spy on Prince John?"

"I would not use the word 'spy'," Robin disagreed. "Just listen for any information you think might be pertinent to us. If you overhear anything, pass it on to Tuck. He will see it gets to me."

"Is there a reason I cannot give it to you directly?" Marian asked.

Robin's voice softened. "I will not risk your safety." He let go of Marian's hands and she felt his fingertips briefly against her cheek.

Marian peered at him in the dim light. "Robin, I—"

He cut her off, placing one hand over her mouth. "Shhh…listen. Someone is coming."

"I was told I could find the Lady Marian inside. Are you quite sure you have not seen her?"

The voice shocked Marian, and she spoke against his palm. "Why is she looking for me?"

"I have no idea," Robin said.

"No, Lady Nyneve," they heard a man's deep voice answer. "But there are many paths. Have you tried looking from one of the bridges?"

"Not yet." The woman's voice quavered. "If you will go check and come find me in the castle afterward, that would be most helpful. I fear my aged bones are aching more than usual today."

"As you like." The deep voice responded. Both voices faded as they moved farther away from Robin and Marian's hiding place.

Robin removed his hand from Marian's mouth and quirked an eyebrow. "Why is Nyneve looking for you?"

"Maybe she is trying to find Father," Marian said. "I cannot think of why else she would care about me."

Robin pushed the honeysuckle aside and gestured Marian before him. "I asked her once to join the Merry Men, but she just laughed at me. Said she was here to watch history, not make it. She is a bit odd, but harmless."

Marian squinted in the daylight. "But why would a historian need to see me? What could I possibly tell her?"

"That is an interesting question to ask of a friar."

Marian whirled around and came face to face with the owner of the voice, who stepped backwards.

"Peace, child." White gold hair flowed over the slightly stooped shoulders of an old woman. Gray eyes so light they looked sun bleached met Marian's. "I have been looking for the friar on a matter of some importance." A slight smile curved her lips. "I am afraid I used your name as an excuse to search the maze, Lady Marian. I do hope you will forgive me, but I need to speak with him without your presence."

"Marian knows who I am, Nyneve," Robin stated. "She can stay, if she wishes."

The old woman shook her head. "I am afraid I must insist on privacy, 'Friar'. This matter is too important."

Robin turned to Marian. "I am sorry we could not spend our time more pleasantly, Marian."

Marian's cheeks flushed at the way his voice caressed her name. "So am I."

"All right, you have said your farewells, lovebirds. You can pledge your troth later. Robin, pull your cowl up. Lady Marian, go away." Nyneve took Robin's arm and lead him away, leaving Marian to stand in the maze, alone.

The honeysuckle brushed against the shoulders of Marian's gown. Whatever other name Robin called it, she had just agreed to spy on the Sheriff of Nottingham and the Prince of England. Suddenly, the quiet of the maze was too quiet. Her skin began to crawl as she imagined others, more influential than her, doing what she had agreed to do...but with her family as the target. And it was obvious Mother and Father had secrets to hide; secrets they did not want anyone else to know about. There was only one place Marian could gather her thoughts without being bothered; one place where no-one would look for her.

Chapter Fifteen:

Marian wrapped her arms around herself and shivered. The castle felt colder than usual. As she headed toward her suite of rooms the echo of childish laughter made her hesitate. It sounded similar to what she had heard the night before. Marian turned toward the sound, following it into a stone hallway as it faded into silence. A single torch sputtered near the entrance to the hall, its flame fighting to stay alive in a black iron holder. She stood on her toes to remove the torch from its sconce. The wall felt cold and slimy when her fingers brushed against it. It had been a long time since anyone had walked through here. Cobwebs hung down from the ceiling like filmy drapes. Marian used the torch to burn them away as she crept further down the dark hall. In front of her was a set of stone stairs leading upward.

"Is she coming?"

"Course she is."

The voices floated down the staircase. Marian stopped and swallowed. Children would never be allowed here. It was the ghosts, it had to be. She swallowed again, heart pounding. Lord Aelfred said they played pranks. No one actually got hurt…did they? Wiping her damp hands on her gown, she forced herself forward. The ghosts were children and had died, alone and afraid. They deserved better treatment in their death then they had received in their life.

Her feet carried her up the curving stone, worn smooth after years of use. Boyish giggles accompanied her progress. She placed one hand against the uneven wall and continued upward until the steps ended at a low doorway.

Marian stepped through and found herself on the battlements. The only sound she could hear was dim footfalls. No doubt it was guards, patrolling their assigned areas. The shadows on the ground grew longer with the setting sun. She shivered again. This was where rumor said the boys had died, their bodies swaying against the walls meant to shield them from harm. A cold chill that did not come from the cooling summer air crawled across her skin.

"*What now?*" A boy's high pitched voice said.

"*Do not worry,*" the other voice answered, "*they will be here soon.*"

"Who—" Marian's voice cracked, and she tried again. "Who is coming?"

More giggles.

"*She is scared of them.*"

"*Shhh.*"

Fading light traced long fingers of gray along the edges of the low walls as the sun finally dropped completely below the horizon.

"*They are coming,*" the voices whispered in unison.

The hair on the back of Marian's neck rose. She tried to swallow, but her mouth had gone dry. The shadows grew longer, stretching across the battlements until they tore themselves free to swirl and eddy around her ankles. She did not move, not even when the shadows separated and coalesced into two forms, one slightly hidden behind the other. The first figure smiled at her, one hand clasping the hand of the child behind him. They were young boys on the cusp of the manhood they would never attain. Marian's eyes welled with sympathetic tears.

"What are you doing here?" She asked.

"*She does not understand.*"

"*They will explain it to her.*" More boyish giggles followed that statement.

The first ghost raised his chin, the beginnings of a downy beard on his nearly transparent cheeks. Marian could see where the rope that hung him had cut into his windpipe. The younger boy stepped out from behind him, lifting his chin so she could see the identical marks across his throat.

"Wh—what do you want?" Marian took a cautious step forward, her hand outstretched to touch him. As her fingers touched his palm, he shimmered briefly. The unnatural shadows laughed.

The boys shrugged in unison, the younger one stepping back to stand next to the older boy, his hand reaching out to clasp the other child's.

As Marian watched, they solidified, their features becoming more distinct. Both ghosts had curly dark hair, wide blue eyes and wore long white shirts which hung to just below their knees.

The eldest one pointed to his throat and shook his head.

"You cannot speak? But—I've heard the other ones..."

The boys sighed, chests rising and falling with breath they no longer had. Opening their mouths wide, they screamed wordlessly.

A screeching so ghastly it threatened to uproot Marian's very soul emerged from the ghosts' mouths. She dropped to her knees, her hands covering her ears. The sound faded away and Marian raised her head, eyes watering.

"I do not understand," she said.

The youngest one pulled his hand free of the other boy and, with a wink, began to sink into the stone directly in front of her. When he was buried nearly up to his chest, he raised one ethereal hand and beckoned her closer.

Marian took a cautious step forward, but as she did, he sank further into the stone until he disappeared entirely, leaving her staring at the ghost who remained. The young boy opened his mouth and she cringed, waiting to hear his unearthly shriek. He sighed, a barely felt puff of air against her face, and vanished into the stone, his hand gesturing her to follow him.

"Wait!" she cried, "I do not understand what you want."

Marian heard the soft metallic sound of chain mail approaching and turned.

"My lady, what are you doing here?" A single guard, his face worn and leathery, walked toward her, his footsteps slow and methodical.

"I—needed some fresh air," Marian said.

"You came up here for some air?" The astonishment in his voice was plain, and Marian stared at him. "But—no-one comes up here. Ever."

"Why not? Is it dangerous?" She glanced over at the edge of the castle. "The walls seem sound enough."

"It is the ghosts, my lady." He ran one hand across his graying beard and lowered his voice. "It is said they are strongest here, where they were killed."

"I did hear voices," Marian admitted. "But I thought nothing of it."

The guard shook his head. "You should not be up here." He glanced around. "Never know what might happen."

"So the ghosts are real, then?" Marian followed the guard across the battlements to a staircase winding down the side of the castle to the grounds below.

"Real enough. Watch your step. These was the stairs those poor boys climbed for the hanging."

Marian hugged the wall as they began the steep climb down. It was a long drop. "Why did they die?"

The guard stopped walking and turned on the staircase to face her. "They were innocent boys," he said. "And I was not here when it happened."

It was an interesting response. "What about others? Why is no-one else curious about them?"

"Milady, if you are not careful, you will fall." The guard said, ignoring her question. "A few of the boys slipped on their way up here that night."

"If you were not here, how do you know that?" Marian asked.

He stepped up one stair to place a hand at her elbow. "I never said I was not in the castle. Just not here." He leaned close. "These are dangerous questions. If you could get into the dungeons, you might find some answers."

Marian drew in breath to answer, but he shook his head. "Now, as I said, watch your step."

"How would I access the dungeons?"

He helped her down the last step, and then turned to face her again. "You would not. It is not meant for the likes of you."

"But you said—"

"I said *if* you could. I did not say you could." He glared at her for a moment before turning swiftly and marching off.

Marian had no idea what the ghosts were trying to tell her, and the guard knew more than he was willing to admit. As much as she wanted to speak to Friar Tuck and through him to Robin, it was time for bed. Marian glanced around her. She could see corn stalks, waving lazily in the moonlit vegetable gardens. She would have to find her way around to the front of the castle in the dark, and then to her rooms.

Chapter Sixteen:

"What do you know about the dungeons?" Marian seated herself next to Tuck on the marble bench.

Friar Tuck squinted at her in the bright morning light. "Is there something specific you want to know?"

Marian glanced around the courtyard. It was early enough that the only people visible were the ever present guards and a few servants. Nevertheless, she lowered her voice to a near whisper.

"One of the guards told me if I wanted answers about the ghosts, I should look in the dungeons. Do you know what he meant?"

Tuck shrugged. "I do not know why he would tell you that. The boys were not kept in the dungeons."

"Were you here when they died?" Marian asked.

The friar turned toward her. "They did not just die, Lady Marian. They were killed. Never forget that."

"But...*why* were they killed? It seems as though no-one knows."

"Only one person knows the real reason they were hung," Tuck said. "Prince John himself. All anyone knows for sure is that they were marched up to their deaths, one after the other, straight from their beds. Most of the people believe he simply grew tired of holding so many boys hostage to their father's good behavior. Oh, the boys' fathers were told a different story, one of betrayal and treason to the throne, but not one of them dared exact vengeance. Not with Richard gone."

"So he just—gets away with murder?"

"He is not the first monarch to have done so," Tuck said mildly. "Even King Arthur used the holy blade, Excalibur, to hold his throne."

"I would hardly equate Prince John with King Arthur." Marian sniffed. "Though the prince seems to believe Excalibur exists and is somewhere in Britain."

"That is interesting. What do you believe?"

"I am not sure," Marian admitted. "It is fantastical, if it is true."

"It is your history. Are you telling me you do not believe it?" Tuck asked.

"I believe the sword existed at one time," Marian said. "But to believe it still exists stretches credibility, do you not agree?"

Tuck shrugged. "There are older swords in the throne room. What makes you think Excalibur cannot exist?"

"Do you think it does?" Marian shifted on the bench.

"I am not saying that," Tuck said. "But you cannot discount the possibility simply because it is an ancient weapon. Next time you walk through the castle, pay close attention to the walls. You will see what I mean."

"Lady Marian? I did not expect t—to find you here."

Marian glanced up to see Aelfred.

Tuck rose to his feet immediately. "I should go." He nodded at the other man. "I have missed seeing you during morning prayers."

The lord flushed. "My father does not—"

"Believe in the strength of prayer, though I had hoped he might have changed his mind since his wife passed." Tuck finished. "I know, but you both are welcome to partake of worship nonetheless."

"Thank you, Friar. I will pass the message t—to my father when I visit him."

"Lady Marian, it is always a pleasure to speak with you." Tuck nodded at her before striding away.

Aelfred shifted from foot to foot. "Will you join me for a walk around the gardens?"

Marian smiled at him. "I would be glad to." She rose to her feet.

"Are you enjoying your st—tay?"

"It has been interesting," Marian said. "I met the ghosts you told me about last night."

"You actually saw them?" Aelfred glanced down at her.

Marian nodded. "Only two," she said. "I think they were brothers."

"Those are the only ones who ever appear," Aelfred said. He pushed an overhanging branch away from the path, releasing it once they'd passed by. "Did you hear the shadows?"

A shiver ran up Marian's spine. "Are those the…the boys, too?"

"Yes, they c—cannot manifest c—completely," Aelfred said. "So they do not bother."

They rounded a curve in the path and Marian gasped in delight. Ahead of them, just off the path in a small clearing, stood a gazebo, blooming honeysuckle climbing up the sides toward the skies. Aelfred took Marian's arm, tucking it into the crook of his elbow. "C—care to sit with me? I have something important t—to ask you."

Marian glanced at him questioningly, but did as he asked. Once she was seated, Aelfred stood in front of her, shifting from foot to foot before he spoke in a rush. "Lady Marian, I know we just met, and I am quite a bit your elder, but would you do me the honor of allowing me t—to c—court you?"

Marian stared at him, not sure what to say. She opened her mouth, then shut it again. Many girls in town had married men years their elder, but she had never expected it to be a possibility for her.

He stepped backward. "I have obviously over-stepped my bounds," he said. "If you will exc—cuse me…" He turned away.

"No! I mean, wait!" Marian blurted. "I am just—you surprised me, that is all."

Aelfred turned back to her, a smile lighting his otherwise homely face. "So you are—not disgusted by the idea?"

"I have a suitor back home," she began carefully. "And it would be unfair of me to lead you on when I shall be returning to him soon."

His face fell. "But your father gave his permission…Why would he do that if you are committed elsewhere?"

"It is—" she paused. "It is—complicated."

"And a secret, I t—take it."

Marian bit her bottom lip, but did not answer.

Aelfred lowered his voice. "You c—can t—trust me, Lady Marian." He grimaced before continuing. "Not many people pay attention t—to someone like me."

"He is not a bad man," Marian said. "But my parents would never approve of him."

"Then allow me the pleasure of simply k—keeping you c—company while you are here." He smiled. "I know how lonely it c—can get."

Marian smiled back. "I would like that very much."

"May I join you?" He waited for Marian's nod before seating himself next to her on the marble bench.

"T—tell me more of this secret beau of yours," he said. "When did you meet him?"

"It is not very interesting," Marian deflected. "Will you tell me more about what growing up here has been like?"

Aelfred shrugged. "Is there something specific you wanted t—to know?"

"Just...everything." Marian laughed. "I am sorry I am not being very clear. Most of the time this place makes me feel like a country bumpkin."

"Are you sure it is the place, and not the people?"

"It is the people, too," she admitted. "Everyone is so sophisticated and beautiful all the time."

"Only because we are bored st—tiff," Aelfred said. "C—court was different when the k—king was here."

Marian leaned toward him. "I have heard that before," she said. "What do you mean?"

'It is not appropriate for me t—to speak ill of the prince. But he runs Nottingham C—castle the same way he would run England."

"Do you mean you do not approve of it?"

"I would like t—to see the k—king back on the throne." Aelfred said. He leaned forward. "I know you have a suitor back home, but I simply c—cannot help myself." Without warning, he captured Marian's lips with his own.

Marian pushed him away. "Lord Aelfred, what are you doing?! I am spoken for!"

The man leapt to his feet, his face flaring. "I am so sorry, Lady Marian! I have no idea what c—came over me!"

"I think you need to leave," Marian said.

"Of c—course," Aelfred agreed. He bowed once before hurrying off.

Marian touched her lips with her fingers. Aelfred's kiss was quite unlike Robin's had been, and wholly inappropriate considering the difference in their ages, but not entirely unpleasant, and his views of Prince John seemed to be the same as hers. He could not possibly be her beau, the kiss notwithstanding, but there was the possibility he could be an ally of sorts. It was something to consider.

Chapter Seventeen:

"So you have found a suitor?"

Marian squealed and leapt to her feet as Robin strolled around the corner, still hidden in his mock friar's robes.

"What on earth? Are you spying on me?" She crossed her arms over her chest and glared at him.

"No, but I was coming to find you," Robin replied. "I just did not expect to find you kissing someone else."

"I was not kissing him. He was kissing me."

Robin raised one eyebrow. "So I noticed." He stepped forward, taking Marian's hands and tugging her closer. "Either way, I did not like it."

"Robin, what if someone sees us?" Marian tried to pull back, to no avail.

"All they will see will be a friar, comforting a young woman who feels lost because of her first foray at court." He grinned.

She smiled back. "You seem to have thought of everything."

"You are not serious about allowing Lord Aelfred to court you, are you?"

Marian blushed. "No, he is far too old. Besides, I told him I already have a suitor."

Robin's arms slid around Marian's waist. "And you do, at that," he murmured before bending his head to hers and capturing her willing lips with his.

After a long, endless moment, she pushed at his chest. "But what are you doing here?"

"The Lady Nyneve sent me to find you."

"The historian? But—why?"

"She did not tell me. I have instructions, however, to bring you to the chapel. Immediately."

"Then should we not go?" Marian asked.

"I do not think she will mind if we delay our arrival," Robin drawled, still holding her in the circle of his arms.

Marian thought of the historian, and silently disagreed with Robin's assessment. The old woman scared her. But the fear did not stop her from snuggling deeper into Robin's warm embrace. She rested her head against the scratchy woolen robe and sighed.

"I wish I could just go home," she said softly. "Being here is complicated."

Robin reached up and brushed a strand of hair away from her face. "I know it is very different from town," he started, but Marian interrupted him.

"It is more than that, Robin. It is this feeling I have that Mother and Father are hiding something important from me. And I saw two ghosts last night on the battlements. They acted as though they needed to tell me something, but I have no idea what."

"Complicated, indeed."

"Oh, there is something I think you should know," Marian continued. "Prince John is very interested in the sword of King Arthur."

Robin nodded. "Tuck already told me," he said. "John does not think you have it, does he?"

Marian tilted her head back to gaze up at him. "He asked me about it, but, quite honestly, I had no idea what he was talking about."

"Your mother never told you about Camelot?" Robin asked.

"Mother and I do not speak much," Marian said. "She never seemed to find much use for me. I think I act too masculine for her tastes."

Robin kissed the top of Marian's head. "I am sure that is not entirely true." He pressed her to him once more before stepping away. "Come, we should go. The Lady Nyneve is tolerant of me, but I do not wish to put that tolerance to the test."

It was a quiet walk to the chapel. Marian kept pace with Robin, but a few steps behind, so as to not attract unwanted attention. A few of the guards glanced at them as they hurried past, but Robin ensured his cowl was pulled up and they did not say a word.

Robin pulled the wooden doors open, allowing Marian to enter before him. The chapel itself was cool and dark, its only light filtering through a small stained glass window above the altar. Dust motes spiraled toward the high wooden ceiling.

"I do not understand why you asked us all here," Mother was seated in the first row of pews, Father at her side.

"Marian, do come in and take a seat. You too, Friar. Be sure to lock the door behind you, if you please. We need to have a private conversation."

Robin nodded, doing as she bade him.

"Will you *please* tell us what this is all about?" Mother sounded impatient, but she patted Marian's hand reassuringly as Marian sat down beside her.

"You always were impatient," Nyneve turned away from the altar and faced the pews.

"But this is serious business, Beatrix." She pinned Mother with her glare. "What were you thinking, bringing it here?"

"I have no idea what you are referring to," Mother said.

Nyneve stepped forward until she was face to face with Mother. "Do not pretend with me. I am far more skilled at pretense than you. Now, tell me. Where did you hide Excalibur?"

Before Marian could react to the old historian's words, Mother had lunged forward, her hands wrapped around Nyneve's throat.

"How could you possibly know about that?" Mother growled; her voice was low and dangerous.

"Mother! What are you doing?" Marian pulled frantically at Mother's fingers. "You are going to kill her! Let go."

"Beatrix, think about what you are doing," Father's rich voice was calm and soothing.

Mother slowly loosened her hold on the old woman.

Nyneve coughed. "That is all right," she rasped. "I should have known better than to provoke her."

"What are you talking about?" Marian said.

"Really, Beatrix? Have you refused to confide in your daughter?" Nyneve rubbed her throat.

"I keep my daughter informed of anything that pertains to her," Mother responded, her voice still hard. "That will not change."

"Wrong," Nyneve's voice mirrored Mother's in its strength. "It will change. It must, because of your actions."

"*My* actions?" Mother spat out. "I do not know how you gathered the information you apparently have, but what you believe you know is wrong."

Nyneve straightened and, it looked to Marian, gained stature as she did so. "My entire life has been about ensuring that blade did not fall into the wrong hands. What were you *thinking*?"

"You mean...Excalibur is real?" Marian finally said. She glanced at Robin, who had remained standing by the doors. He shrugged.

"Of course it is real, you have been training with it for years," Nyneve said.

"I—what?" Marian turned to Mother. "Is that true?"

Mother held up one hand. "Wait, Marian." She glared at Nyneve. "How do you know about the sword?"

"I am its original guardian." The old historian swiftly knotted her long white gold hair into a knot at the base of her neck.

"You cannot be," Mother said. "That is—"

"—ancient history? Yes, I know." Nyneve said. "Nevertheless, here I am. And, thanks to your ham-handedness, so is the sword."

"Listen, if you are The Lady of the Lake, you would understand there is no way I would have left that sword behind. It is too much of a temptation." Mother growled back. "Now, prove who you are before I kill you with my bare hands."

"What proof would you accept?"

"Tell me something only the du Luc family knows," Mother demanded.

"I know," Nyneve said slowly, "what secrets the lake Llyn Trawsfynydd holds."

Mother fell back a step, knees pushed up against the wooden edge of the pew. Her face was white.

Nyneve nodded. "Interestingly enough, that is also where I was killed."

"But," Mother whispered, staring at the old woman, "that happened centuries ago."

"Five centuries, to be somewhat inexact," Father interjected.

"Correct, Alan," Nyneve said. "You know my history well."

"What secrets is she talking about?" Marian asked.

Nyneve glared at Mother again. "Did you teach her *nothing*?"

"Lady Nyneve, enough." Father spoke. "If Marian knows little of our family history, blame me. Beatrix had—other concerns."

"Yes, Robin told me of them," Nyneve said.

Mother, Father and Marian all looked at Robin, who moved away from the doors, pulling his cowl down as he did so.

"What is your part in this?" Mother asked.

"How do you know Mother?" Marian queried at the same time.

Robin raised both his hands in a gesture of surrender. "Lady Beatrix," he began, but she cut him off.

"You involved my daughter in your Merry Men schemes?!"

Robin's tone was as unrepentant as his answer. "Well, you were not using her."

"It is not a joke, Robin!" Mother snapped. "You had no business doing it. It was not your right!"

"She could get me information you could not," Robin said. "You were not willing to use your station to get near the prince, so I found another source."

Marian blinked. "You worked for Robin, Mother?"

"I worked *with* him, not for him. Now quit interrupting, Marian."

"I am not a child. Stop treating me as one." Marian's voice was firm. "I think I deserve some answers. From everyone." Her glare included Robin.

"Very well," Father said. "What exactly do you want to know?"

"Have you been working with him, too?" Marian asked. She folded her arms across her chest.

"Only indirectly," Father admitted. "I would hear rumors and pass them to Robin when I could. I understand you are upset at everyone, Mari, but this is truly for the best. What we have been doing has been for the best."

"So you are telling me that lying to me my entire life has been for 'the best'?" Her voice shook.

"It was not all lies," Mother began, but Marian interrupted her.

"It certainly was not the truth, either!"

"Marian, lower your voice," Nyneve instructed. "We have a modicum of privacy here, but these walls are not meant for yelling."

"Sorry," Marian murmured.

"Now, everyone needs to calm down," Nyneve continued. "I know it is a lot to take in and yes, Marian, I shall answer as many of your questions as I can. First of all, I think *proper* introductions are in order." She straightened and the air itself seemed to gather around her in a light haze. "I am known simply as the historian of Nottingham now, but I was once the Lady of the Lake, and before that I was Queen Nyneve, wife of King Ban and mother of Lancelot du Luc."

"Lancelot, as in King Arthur's Lancelot?" Robin said curiously.

Nyneve cocked one silver eyebrow at him. "As far as I know, there has only been one," she said.

"You mentioned secrets about Llyn Trawsfynydd." Marian said. "What secrets did you mean?"

The old woman sighed. "You really did not tell her, Beatrix?"

Mother shook her head. "It did not seem relevant to her life."

"Very well, then. Marian, Robin, have a seat. You too, Beatrix, though you already know the story." The haze at Nyneve's feet wrapped around her white gown, making it glow with an inner light. "Llyn Trawsfynydd is an ancient place," she began when everyone seated themselves in the pew, Robin taking a seat next to Marian. "Even in my time, it was a place of great power and gatherings." She stared at their faces for a moment, then shook herself and continued. "Let me begin again. What does each of you know of Merlin Ambrosis?"

"Merlin Ambrosis is ancient history, Nyneve." Mother objected. "Do you mean to drag out the whole story here and now?"

"Of course not," Nyneve said. "Very well. Suffice it to say, Merlin was a wizard of King Arthur's court; some say the greatest wizard, but that is not important. Not really."

"I remember hearing stories of him," Marian said. "Was he killed in a battle at…" her voice trailed off.

The Lady of the Lake nodded. "Yes, that is correct. The battle took place at Llyn Trawsfynydd. But he did not die, not completely. We managed to kill his body and trap his spirit for all eternity."

"We? You mean you were there?" Marian asked again.

"Yes. My son's daughter and I captured him and poured his essence into the lake." She shrugged. "It was a fitting punishment for his crimes."

"His crimes?" Robin leaned forward. "But he was the greatest wizard Britian's ever known."

"He was a misguided fool." Nyneve said bluntly. "But I digress. This is not about Merlin. It is about the secrets of the lake. And I have told you one. The other is not for you to know."

Marian opened her mouth to say something, but a pounding at the chapel door interrupted her.

Chapter Eighteen:

"Why is this door locked?? Open it at once!" The sheriff's voice came through the wooden doors clearly.

Marian looked at Robin, eyes wide. "You cannot be found here!"

"The passageway," Nyneve directed. "Now, Robin. Hurry."

Robin pressed a quick kiss to one of Marian's hands before he scrambled out of the pew and ran toward the back of the chapel.

"But—there's nothing back there," she protested.

Father's hand on her shoulder prevented her from rising. "He'll be fine, Mari."

A barely seen flick of Robin's wrist, and Marian watched as a panel of stone slid halfway open. Without a backward glance Robin slipped through it and the panel turned to become a smooth stone wall once more.

"Break the doors down!" The sheriff ordered.

"Sheriff," Nyneve called out, "there's no need for such theatrics. I am coming." Her voice suddenly shook and the glow around her dissipated until it vanished entirely. Moving more slowly than before, she walked to the doors and undid the bolt holding them shut. "Come in, sheriff."

The sheriff and three guardsmen pushed their way into the chapel.

"Why were the doors barred, historian?"

"I am not under your jurisdiction, sheriff," Nyneve said coldly. "An amount of courtesy is due me."

"This is my home," growled the sheriff. "You are here at Prince John's suffrage, which means you are here at mine, as well."

"You overstep yourself," the Lady retorted. "And the doors were barred at my insistence. If you have issue with it, take it up with King Richard upon his return. I have violated none of the liberties he conferred upon me."

"King Richard is not here," the sheriff stated. "I am."

The Lady glared at him. "Indeed you are. But I have done nothing wrong, sheriff, simply barred a door you did not wish barred."

The sheriff stared at her for a moment before turning to where Marian sat. "Lady Marian, Lady Beatrix, are you all right?"

"Yes," Marian said.

"All three of us are fine," Mother said. "But your concern is unnecessary. Was there something in particular you needed?"

The man shook his head. "I became concerned when I could not find Lady Marian," he said. "I very much would like to accompany her to dinner."

"Marian will be seated with us." Father said. "Come, Marian, Beatrix. Lady Nyneve, it was a pleasure to speak with you. I certainly hope we can do it again sometime soon." He rose to his feet, Mother and Marian followed suit.

"I *am* feeling a bit tired, and we need to change before dinner." Mother said. The woman Marian had seen earlier was gone as though she'd never existed.

"I will join you as soon as I am able," Nyneve said calmly. "I look forward to sitting with you tonight."

Marian felt the sheriff's stare boring into her back on the short walk to the chapel doors.

"He is too arrogant for my comfort," Mother fumed as they walked across the cobblestones. "He has designs on you, Mari, and I do not like it."

"Bea, you need to keep your temper under control," Father warned. "We're not safe here."

"Do you think I do not know that?" Mother snapped, and then apologized. "I am sorry, Alan. You're right, of course. Marian, where is Anna? Did not I tell you she needed to be with you at all times?"

"She refused to set foot in the gardens again, Mother. Not once she saw the maze." Marian said. "What was I supposed to do? Sit in the kitchens with her?"

Mother's voice was cool and refined, a far cry from what Marian had witnessed in the chapel. "What a silly girl. If I'd known she was so flighty, I would never have brought her. There are perfectly beautiful gardens that are not confined by trees and such." She shrugged. "I cannot blame you for her faults, however. I will have words with her upon her return. It is not fitting that you should do without a ladies' maid because she is fearful of close spaces."

"I was speaking with Friar Tuck in the gardens earlier," Marian said. "I hardly think I needed a ladies' maid for that."

"You need a ladies' maid for everything, Mari. I told you that before we came."

"I did not think you still meant it, now that," Marian glanced around her and lowered her voice, "I know the truth."

Mother grabbed her arm with enough force that Marian winced. "Not here," she hissed. "Our rooms will be safer."

"But—what about spies?" Marian asked.

Mother snorted as she stifled a laugh. "Spies are less prevalent than you think," she said. "The kind you're thinking of, skulking around halls and such, are few and far between. Most spies are just people in the right place at the right time."

"Not quite," Father muttered under his breath.

Mother smirked at him as she swept past him and into the hallway leading to their rooms.

"Am I missing something?" Marian asked, following her parents.

"A private jest, and not one worth mentioning," Mother said.

"Oh, I do not know, Bea," Father scratched his chin. "I think it is worth telling."

Mother sighed, but Marian could tell it was not in true exasperation. "It was not anything serious." She pulled open the door to their suite.

Marian waited until the door shut behind all three of them before saying anything. "But what happened?"

Father plopped down on the closest couch. "Your mother, whom I love dearly, nearly scared me to death my first night in Nottingham."

"What? How?" Marian curled up in the recliner across from him, dragging a soft woolen blanket across her lap.

"Your father," Mother said briskly, "exaggerates. He was not frightened, merely startled by my unexpected appearance."

"You were soaking wet!" Father said. "Up to your knees, soaked through. What was I supposed to think?"

"Not that I was there to murder you," Mother returned, seating herself next to him.

"Really, Mother? Why were you wet? What were you doing?" Marian looked from one to the other, eyes wide.

"I had been contracted to spy on someone specific," Mother said. "It was sheer misfortune that I counted the window panes wrong and wound up in his rooms by mistake."

"It was not misfortune," Father said. "If you had not done that, I would never have had the courage to approach you in open court."

Mother smiled at him and it lit her entire face. "I am glad you did."

"But how long were you a spy?" Marian interrupted.

"Since shortly after my arrival at King Henry's court," Mother said. "Excalibur made me better with a sword than I would have been under normal circumstances, even with training. Henry valued that, but could not use me as part of his guard, for obvious reasons. So he had me trained as his personal spy instead."

"And you continued doing that?" Marian asked. "Even after you met Father?"

"For a short time," Mother said. "But I left that life when I knew I was going to be a mother. I did not want to raise you in that lifestyle, but I could not quite bring myself to give it up entirely. Not once Prince John came to power." She met Marian's eyes. "I am very, very proud of you for choosing your own path, though my anger at Robin for involving you in his schemes is very real."

"It was not Robin's fault," Marian protested. "It was entirely my idea."

"Somehow I doubt that," Mother said. "But it is far too late to argue further about it. Now we all have to live with our choices."

"Somehow I think Lady Nyneve will have a hand in those choices," Father interjected. "She seems to be a force of nature."

"You know what she is better than anyone else," Mother said. "How many songs have you written about The Lady of the Lake and Camelot?"

"More than I can count," Father said. "The real question, Bea, is what are we going to do about the sword?"

Mother sighed. "It is Marian's, just as it was mine and my mother's before me." She met Marian's gaze. "So the question becomes, what are you going to do about the sword, Marian?"

Marian gulped. "Me?"

"You." Mother said. "It is your responsibility now."

"Bea, that is hardly fair," Father complained.

"This is the life she chose, Alan. While I am proud of her choices, now she needs to learn what they are all about."

"Ummm..." Marian bit her bottom lip as she thought. "I think the sword should go back to Nyneve. It was hers originally, and she seemed very angry at you for bringing it here."

Mother nodded. "That is a very responsible decision, Marian. You can inform the Lady of your decision over dinner. Just ensure you are not overheard."

"No, I mean yes. I mean, I will make sure."

"Then that takes care of that," Mother said. She rose. "Now we need to dress for dinner. It would not do to be late. We do not need the sheriff attempting to break down our suite door in his eagerness for your company."

Marian giggled at the idea, then calmed when she remembered the chapel. If a place of God was not safe from the sheriff, no-where would be. It was a sobering thought.

"Anna has not returned from the kitchens, so I will help you dress," Mother said. "Alan, if you will excuse us?"

"Of course," Father agreed.

Marian and Mother walked into the other set of rooms. "We should not be too long," Mother threw back over her shoulder.

"I will wait out here." Father said. He crossed his legs at the ankles and closed his eyes.

"He is not...sleeping, is he?" Marian asked quietly.

"No, he is probably just composing his next ballad. He says he can concentrate more in perfect quiet."

Marian nodded and closed the door behind them.

Chapter Nineteen:

"You look lovely." The sheriff greeted Marian as she walked into the dining hall with Mother and Father.

"Thank you, sheriff," Marian returned smoothly. Mother had put Guinevere's jeweled comb in her hair, and she truly did feel lovely.

"Prince John has requested your presence at his table," he continued, including Mother and Father in the thinly veiled order. "The Lady Nyneve is already seated there."

Marian threw a glance at her parents. Father nodded minutely at her in a silent reply.

"Thank you, sheriff," Mother said. "We would be honored."

"Lady Marian, can I hope you might be seated next to me?" The sheriff asked.

"I did not realize you'd be joining us, sheriff." Marian said.

"I always take my meals with His Highness," the sheriff replied. "My place is at his side."

"So I see," Marian murmured, but quietly enough that he did not hear her.

With the sheriff leading the way, they wound their way to the prince's table and took their seats next to Nyneve, who winked at Marian.

"Lady Marian, Lady Beatrix, Alan, we are glad to see you are well." The prince took a bite of cheese as he spoke. "The sheriff tells me you spent some time in the chapel today?"

Mother nodded. "It is a quiet place to think." She tittered. "I am afraid my time spent away from court dulled my senses to all the entertainments you have provided."

The prince narrowed his eyes. "If that was truly the case, why did you have a need to bar the doors, thus keeping everyone else in need of prayer outside?"

"As I told the sheriff," Nyneve interrupted, "that was entirely my doing. There was no reason to bring it to your attention."

"Any time a door is barred in *my* castle, it is deserving of my attention. I am regent during my brother's absence, Lady Nyneve. It would not service you well to misremember that."

"You forget yourself, Your Highness," the old woman replied calmly. "My loyalty is to the throne, not the one who sits in it. I have been Nottingham's historian since before your father ruled, and my current duties allow me certain freedoms you, as *regent*, cannot take away."

Much to Marian's shock, the prince bowed his head to the historian. "I know of your importance to my brother. But you still have not answered the question."

"If it is that important to you," Nyenve said, "the answer is simple. I wished for a certain amount of privacy and I closed the doors to ensure it."

"Very well." Prince John turned to his right. "Does that answer suffice, sheriff, or do you still believe Lady Nyneve is telling falsehoods?"

"It is the same thing she told me," the sheriff agreed. "So yes, my prince, the answer is sufficient." He snapped his fingers and a servant standing behind him poured what Marian assumed was wine into his goblet. Taking a long swig, he stared at Marian across the table.

Marian shifted uncomfortably and sipped at her own goblet, trying unsuccessfully to avoid his eyes.

"Did you notice he is here?"

She was not sure if she was the only one who heard the sibilant whispering of multiple boyish voices. No-one else seemed to respond. Marian glanced at the prince. His face had bleached to a color resembling Mother's wedding gown and his hand, as he reached for his goblet, shook slightly.

"He is scared of us. See how he shakes?"

"He should be," the first voice said. *"He killed us."*

"Enough!" Prince John roared. The hall fell silent and all eyes turned toward him. The ghosts laughed and laughed.

Prince John pushed away from the table. "I shall leave within the week," he announced abruptly. "Sheriff, you will accompany me back to London."

"I—I cannot possibly, Your Highness," the sheriff stuttered.

A small breeze ruffled the collar on Marian's gown. *"He cannot leave,"* a voice whispered in her ear. *"If he does, she will die."*

"Who?" Marian asked, looking around her. "Where is she?"

"We cannot tell you," the little boy's voice said.

"Who are you talking to?" Mother asked.

"You cannot hear it?" Marian turned to face Mother.

Mother shook her head. ."And neither can anyone else. You sound crazed."

"It is the ghosts, Mother." Marian lowered her voice. "Or at least one of them. He told me if the sheriff leaves, someone will die."

"Did he tell you anything else?" Mother's voice was serious. "Like who, or where?"

"All he told me was that she will die."

"Then we have a week to figure out who and where 'she' is." Mother said. She turned to Prince John, who had seated himself again. "Your Highness, does your announcement mean we are released from our duty and can return home?"

A frown crossed the prince's brow. "My request was that you attend me for the duration of my stay. Was that not made perfectly clear to you at the outset?"

"Not exactly," Mother said. "We were simply informed to attend upon your Highness."

"Sheriff, it seems you have been lax in administering our express desires," the prince said. "Our instructions were to issue invitations, not orders."

"I apologize, Your Highness," the sheriff said. Marian could hear the falseness in his words, but Prince John merely nodded.

"Try some peacock, Lady Marian," the prince said. "The eyeballs are particularly tasty."

Marian shuddered. "No, thank you, Your Highness. I am afraid I did not grow up with this type of food. It is taking some getting used to."

Prince John shrugged. "Have the servants bring you something more to your taste, then. We won't have anyone go hungry at our table."

"I will have some vegetable soup and some bread, Highness. Thank you for your concern."

"Are you enjoying your visit here?" The prince asked Marian. "We have not seen very much of you during your stay."

"It has been enlightening," Marian's voice was carefully non-committal.

Prince John laughed. "I do not think anyone has ever called their visit to Nottingham 'enlightening' before now."

"I do not mean to insult you, Your Highness," Marian began, but the prince cut her off.

"I have not been insulted by your words. No, Lady Marian, I find your words refreshing. You are like a freshly picked rose in a vase of dying blooms."

"I—thank you, Your Highness."

The prince nodded and at the sign, musicians Marian could not see began to play softly.

"Lady Marian, would you give me the honor of this dance?" It was more an order than true request, and Marian immediately rose to her feet.

"I would be honored, Your Highness." She put her hand in his and let him lead her to the center of the room.

Chapter Twenty:

"Your mother was quite the figure at court when she lived here," Prince John said, casually spinning her about the dance floor.

"I do not know what you mean, Highness," Marian said. "She never speaks to me of her time here."

"And you are quite sure she never once mentioned Excalibur to you?"

"Yes. I do not even think Mother knows which end of a sword is which."

"Yet I heard a rumor that you are trained with one." The prince observed.

"Father thought it was a good idea," Marian said carefully. "In these times of unrest, and the fact that we live so close to the forest, he believed I should be able to protect myself."

"Very wise of him," the prince said. "And have you had occasion to do that?"

"Do what, Highness?"

"Protect yourself." Prince John kissed the back of her hand before releasing her and Marian realized with a start that the music had ended.

"No, I have only ever practiced with Father."

"Dare I hope you brought your sword with you?"

It was not where Marian expected the conversation to go. "Ummm...I am sorry, Highness. I did not."

"Ah, that is a pity. I have never tried my hand against a female opponent." He snapped his fingers. "But I can provide you with one. What type of blade are you familiar with?"

"The only sword I've used was an old arming sword," Marian admitted.

"An ancient weapon, indeed. Tell me, it is a family blade?"

Marian's heart began to pound. The prince was a master, it seemed, of delving for information. "I do not know, Your Highness. You'd have to ask my parents. All I know is it is the sword I was given."

"Well, I have swords in the armory. My guards can find one for you."

"You want to duel with me, Highness?' Marian asked.

"I believe that is what I have been saying," Prince John returned. "You need not worry. I will go easily on you."

There was no way for her to refuse. Instead, Marian smiled and nodded her agreement. "I look forward to it."

"I will send for you first thing in the morning. We shall duel after we break our fast." His eyes raked over her once. "After I send you some more suitable clothing. I would not wish it said I won unfairly."

He had, Marian noticed, stopped using the royal 'we'. She wondered if it meant something significant about the king's absence. Or his possible return.

"I hate to leave you," Prince John said, "but I have much to do before I return to London. I do hope you enjoy the rest of your evening."

"I—thank you," Marian stuttered.

The prince strode away and the music started up in his absence. Marian glanced around her. Couples were moving onto the floor. She noticed the sheriff striding toward her.

"Lady Marian, I hope you were not leaving," he said as he reached her. "I was looking forward to dancing with you again."

"I was going to stroll through the gardens," Marian said. "I have not had the opportunity to walk through them at my leisure yet."

"If you do not mind, I will join you," the sheriff said. "The gardens are particularly lovely in the moonlight, especially the maze."

"Ummm...I have walked in the maze before. I am afraid it might prove too much of a challenge to get through at night."

The sheriff laughed. "Lady Marian, I was here when that maze was built. I can keep you safe."

"Allow me to be perfectly honest," Marian said, lying through her teeth. "I would rather stay close to the castle until I am more comfortable here."

"Of course. There are perfectly lovely gardens just below the battlements. Would you care to see them?"

"If you mean the vegetable gardens," Marian said, "I have seen them already and while they are abundant, I do not know if I would use the word 'lovely' to describe them."

The sheriff raised one eyebrow. "I did not realize you were so familiar with the grounds."

"I am learning more each day," Marian returned carefully. She scuffed one shoe lightly against the marble floor.

"Well then, since you have already seen the gardens, would you like to join me for a cup of wine?"

Marian shook her head. "I do not drink wine, but a cup of honey mead would be welcome."

The sheriff bowed. "Your wish is my command." He strode across the floor and Marian walked to a nearby chair.

"Are you having fun?" Father startled her and she squeaked.

"I did not see you, Father. I—yes, I suppose I am." She smiled up at him. "Why are not you dancing with Mother?"

Father shrugged. "Your mother is busy holding a court of her own."

Marian looked where Father pointed and giggled. There was Mother, surrounded by courtiers. Interestingly enough, there were very few ladies in the group.

"How does she do that so easily?" Marian asked.

"Do what, exactly?"

"Change personalities like that," Marian said. As she watched, Mother flipped her hair over her shoulder and laughed. "She seems so—so at home."

"This was her home for many, many years," Father pointed out. "She knows what's expected at court; she knows how to play to an audience."

"I do not know who she really is," Marian said. "What I saw in the chapel made me realize what I grew up with was false, but how do I know that was not a front, either?"

"Remember what I told you back home? 'Your mother is who your mother is. No more and no less'? That is the sum of it, Mari. *Both* personalities are true. Just at different times."

"That must get very confusing," Marian stared at Mother.

"Here is your mead," the sheriff said. A tall goblet was thrust at Marian. "What do you find confusing, Lady Marian?"

"Marian was just telling me that she is not used to castle life," Father said. "She finds it overwhelming."

"Exactly," Marian agreed a trifle too quickly.

"Is there anything I can do to put your mind at ease?" The sheriff asked.

"No, I think it will just take some time. But I appreciate your concern." Marian said.

Father smiled at both of them. "I think I will go join your mother. Sheriff, it is always good to see you. Marian, do not forget tomorrow is Sunday. We shall attend service first thing in the morning."

"I will be at the chapel early," she promised.

"You will enjoy the Sunday service," the sheriff told her. "I never miss it. Shall I save you a seat?"

"I would rather sit with my parents," Marian said. The next words almost stuck in her throat, but she forced them out. "But I am sure no-one would object if you joined us."

"Regretfully, I must decline. The prince demands my undivided attention during his visits here."

"Can I ask you something…personal, Sheriff?" Marian placed one hand on his arm and leaned toward him confidentially.

"Of course," he replied.

"Why is Prince John so afraid of the ghosts?"

The sheriff stiffened. "The prince is afraid of nothing," he snapped.

Marian softened her voice further. "He seemed distraught at the noise they were making during dinner."

"They are pests," the sheriff said. "It was nothing more than that."

113

"But what happened to them? Why would they say he killed them?"

"You seem to be very interested in the ghosts of dead children."

"There were dozens of them, Sheriff. How could you *not* be curious?"

"He is not curious because he killed us, too."

The whisper against her ear startled her and she fought not to twitch in response.

"I am not curious, Lady Marian, because they are dead." The sheriff's voice was flat, as though he was talking to her about the weather.

It sent shivers up Marian's spine.

"The ghosts are not a subject I care to discuss," the sheriff continued. "And I suggest you do not bring it up to the prince. He'll view it with less...kindness...than I have."

"My apologies," Marian murmured. "I certainly did not mean any offense."

The sheriff smiled. "None taken. I find you to be quite charming, if a bit unrefined. But I am sure a longer stay here will easily remedy that."

"I believe my parents plan on leaving when the prince does."

"I was not referring to your parents," he said. "I was referring to you."

Marian shook her head. "Oh, but I cannot stay without them. It wouldn't be proper."

"You would be my personal guest. I guarantee nothing would happen to you without my express permission."

She caught the glimmer of madness in his eyes and swallowed. "It is inappropriate for you to even suggest such a thing, Sheriff, and I am not particularly comfortable with where this conversation is going."

"Never mind," the sheriff said. "It is just something for you to consider. After all, it would benefit you greatly to take advantage of your heritage."

"I never even really knew what my heritage *was* until coming here." Marian said. "It simply was not important enough back in town."

"All the more reason for you to stay here. There are plenty of people who would be willing to educate you."

Marian shook her head. "I already told you I was uncomfortable with this conversation, Sheriff."

The sheriff gripped Marian's arm just below the elbow. "Make no mistake, Lady Marian, you are *not* in charge here. I am."

She yanked her arm away from him. "This conversation is *over*." Turning on her heel, she marched away from him on quaking legs. The sheriff, obviously, was no-one to be trifled with. She wondered if Mother could have succeeded where she had failed.

Chapter Twenty-One:

"Where is she going?"

"She does not know."

Marian strode past the stairs leading to her suite. The ghosts were right. She had no idea where she was headed.

"If she does not know, then how is she supposed to get there?"

"If you are not going to speak *to* me, then would you kindly not speak at all?!" Marian snapped aloud.

The ghosts laughed.

"She is feisty; no wonder the sheriff likes her."

"The sheriff is not the only one…"

"Stop it!" Marian commanded them. They did not listen, just giggled harder.

"Do you think she needs a hint?"

"We could give her one," a single, very young, voice replied.

"What are you talking about?" Marian gasped when the shadows which had been clinging to the walls she walked past began shifting and sliding toward her.

"I like her. Let us help." The young ghost announced.

The laughter tapered off and the shadows crowded closer around Marian's skirts.

"Follow us," they whispered. *"It is not too much further."*

Marian shook her head. "This is mad."

The shadows tugged at her skirts, gathering in close, and then stretching farther down the hall. *"You have to hurry,"* they demanded. *"She needs you."*

"She? Who is she?" Following shadows was mad, but the idea of not following them was even crazier.

The ghosts did not answer, just kept undulating back and forth, forcing her further and further down. And the direction she was walking *was* down. The air around her cooled, and the walls, bare now of the shadows which were clinging to the stone floor and her skirts, grew clammy and damp.

Guttering torches placed every few feet did little to relieve the dimness of the long corridor, producing a thick smoke that rose into the air and made her cough. She stepped deeper, taking shallow breaths to keep the smoke from filling her lungs. A skittering sound near her feet caught her attention and she glanced down, stifling a scream as a rat scurried into the flickering shadows the torchlight created against the stone walls.

"Where are you taking me?" She did not really expect an answer.

"*The dungeons,*" was the reply she received. "*That is where she is. That is where she has been.*"

The dust stirred at her feet as she walked and she sneezed. The dust tickled her nose again. She blinked suddenly in surprise. There were footprints on the floor before her and they continued down the corridor for as far as she could see.

"*Why is she slowing down? She needs to walk faster, not slower.*"

"*Leave her alone; she is following us.*"

That was true. She was following them. But where were they leading her? The question so preoccupied her that she barely noticed the wooden doors she walked past until the shadows collected at the last door on the left side of the corridor.

"*There. She is in there.*"

Marian wiped suddenly damp palms against her gown, leaving faint sweaty stains on the light green cotton. She was not sure what was behind the door, but she was equally positive she really did not want to find out.

"*Look at her, she is scared.*" The shadows giggled.

"I am not scared!" Marian said. "I came down here, did not I?"

"*Bet you will not walk through the door,*" the voices taunted.

Marian's spine stiffened and, without hesitation, she twisted the wrought iron handle on the shadow darkened door and stepped inside.

At first glance the room was empty. Torches placed every two feet on the far walls met her gaze. Only two of the torches were lit, throwing flickering shadows on the floor and walls. As Marian watched, the shadow ghosts crawled into the dungeon, coating the floor and the walls with their presence.

"What is this place?" Marian's voice was hushed.

"Are you sure she is not dense? Did not we already tell her?"

"You know, considering I followed you down here, I would think you would be nicer to me," Marian huffed.

"Look around," the shadows directed. *"You will see."*

"I am just a bit tired of being ordered around by shadows," Marian complained.

Laughter.

"H—hello? Is someone there?" The voice was hesitant, and broken, but it was a woman's voice.

Marian took a hesitant step forward. Darkness, a real blackness brought on by lack of torchlight, kept her from walking further.

"P—please, is someone there?"

"Who are you?" Marian peered into darkness, trying to pierce the faint light from the torches.

The woman coughed a dry rasping sound. "Do you have water?"

Marian shook her head before realizing the other woman could not see her. "No, I am sorry."

"It—it does not matter." Marian heard her swallow. "Come closer, so I can see you."

"It is dark," Marian felt stupid as soon as the words left her mouth.

"She is scared of the dark!" *"I thought only babies were scared of the dark!"*

"Hush," the other woman said softly and the ghosts' teasing subsided. "Do not be scared, child." Chains rattled. "I certainly cannot hurt you."

"But," Marian moved closer. "Who are you? Why are you down here?"

The woman laughed. It was more of a wheezing sound than anything Marian thought of as laughter. "The sheriff brought me here as his 'guest' nearly five years ago. He did not want me to leave."

Marian was finally close enough to make out the other woman's features. Greasy brown hair pooled around where she lay, curled into a ball on the cold stone floor. Chains bound both her feet to the closest wall, disappearing under a once fine gown, now stained with water and bits of food.

"Oh, my…what did he do to you?" Marian hurried over, kneeling down by the other woman.

The woman squinted at her. "Do I—know you?"

Marian automatically started shaking her head, then paused. "You almost look like someone I know…"

"I am sure I do not look like anyone anymore. Not even myself."

"Do you have a son?" Marian asked.

"I had a son once," the woman answered on a sigh. "I have not seen him in a very long time. He was twelve or thirteen. A tall boy, nearly as tall as his father."

Marian narrowed her eyes thoughtfully. "What is your name? Do you remember?"

The woman's voice when she replied was sharp. "Of course I remember! The sheriff calls me his Scarlett Bird, you see…and that is my name. Dulcina Scarlett."

Marian gasped. "You are Will's mother!"

Chapter Twenty-Two:

"You know my Will?" Dulcina's voice was dreamy once more. "He is such a good boy. Always behaves and brings me tea."

"I am Marian, Beatrix du Luc's daughter." Marian gazed earnestly into Dulcina's eyes. "Do you not remember me?"

Dulcina bit her lip hard enough to draw blood. "Marian," she said, her voice lucid. "I remember you. You taught Will how to skip stones, much to your mother's dismay."

"*She is not right in the head,*" a ghost whispered in Marian's ear. "*It is the sheriff's fault. He made her sick.*"

"I have no idea how to get you free," Marian admitted. "But we have to get out of here."

Dulcina shook her head. "If I leave, he will get mad at me."

"If you leave, he will not be able to find you," Marian stated. "I can make sure you get back home."

It was odd. She could almost see Dulcina's eyes glaze over. "Where is home, the Scarlett Bird sings. She shivers and shakes and spreads her wings."

"She is mad," Marian muttered under her breath. "What in the Lord's name did he *do* to her?"

"Bad things, scary things; all things we will talk about. You need to help her."

Marian nodded. "Of course I will. I am just...not sure how."

"Better figure it out quick. He is coming."

"The sheriff? Here? Now?"

"*Go further in,*" the ghosts instructed. "*Hide behind the chests.*"

Marian did not hesitate. So far the ghosts had not been wrong about anything; she was not going to take the chance that they might be now. One corner of the room held large chests, stacked deep and high. If she hid behind them and was very still, the sheriff might not notice her. She picked up her skirts and ran, sliding into the miniscule space between the chests and the wall as the bolt on the door began to rise.

"How is my Scarlett Bird?" The honeyed voice she had done her best to ignore over dinner was followed by the door slamming shut.

Dulcina giggled. "I know a secret," she sing-songed. "But I cannot tell you until Will comes back with my tea."

"A secret? What kind of a secret?" The sheriff asked.

Marian risked raising her head a trifle above the chests, barely daring to breathe. Dulcina raised one hand, placing her index finger against her lips. "Shhhh... I cannot tell yet."

The sheriff's shoulders raised and fell as he sighed. "Important things are happening, Scarlett Bird. Very important things." He leaned down and gently touched her cheek with one gloved hand. "Then we can live as we were meant to." He straightened up, moving away from her and touching the torch in his hand to ones on the wall she was chained against until the room blazed with light. He placed the last torch in the empty holder. "There, that is better."

Marian noticed the shadows crowding the edge of the torchlight. The ghosts were not the only ones; Dulcina shrank back as well, as though light touching her would cause her pain.

The sheriff's voice gentled to a near whisper. "I am sorry you have had to stay down here, dearest. It will not be much longer. I promise."

Marian clamped a hand across her own mouth to prevent her gasp of surprise from escaping.

"I need my son," the woman said. "When is Will getting here? I am thirsty."

"He will be here soon," the sheriff promised. "But I brought you water." The man knelt next to her and gathered her into his embrace. "Here, drink this." He held a flask up to her lips. "Tell me something, my love... tell me your secret."

Dulcina gulped at the water running down her chin. "The ghosts know," she said. "They know everything." She gazed up at him earnestly. "Did you know that? Did you know they know everything?"

The sheriff shook his head, a look of sheer frustration crossing his features.

"*He broke her. She will never be right again.*"

Marian was mesmerized by the scene playing out in front of her. It was obvious the sheriff loved Dulcina; loved her almost to the point of distraction.

"They are here," Dulcina blurted out. "They came by carriage and horse and they are here. Did they bring Will? Is he with them?"

"Hush, Scarlett Bird," the sheriff said. "No-one is here, no-one came."

"NO!" The other woman screamed. "You are wrong! The ghosts saw them! They told me!"

"Prince John is here," he tried to soothe her, but she twisted in his arms before suddenly quieting.

"It is Beatrix du Luc and Alan a Dale." Dulcina's voice went calm. "Have you met their daughter yet? She and Will are friends."

"Yes, I have met them. They arrived last week," the sheriff said. "It is all right. Just rest, Scarlett Bird, nothing will hurt you down here."

"Nothing except him. Look at her hand; look at her palm."

"Marian is a sweet child," Dulcina continued. "I think she and Will might marry some day. But that is a long way off. They are children."

"Of course they are," the sheriff agreed. "Is that the secret the ghosts told you?"

Dulcina smiled. "What else would it be? Did you bring me food?"

He shook his head. "A guard will bring some down soon. Would you like to change your gown today?"

"No, why should I?" She smoothed the stained fabric over her breast. "Is it not lovely?"

"It is, but you wore it for dinner. It is nearly time for supper."

"Oh, then I suppose that is fine." Dulcina said. "But you cannot help me. That would not be proper."

The sheriff smiled, a genuine one that lit the part of his face Marian could see. "I will go and send someone down to help you change. Would that be all right?"

"You are so good to me." She reached up to touch his face and Marian caught the glimmer of...something...on the palm of her hand.

He grabbed Dulcina's hand and pressed a kiss against her palm before double checking the chains that held her to the wall. "I will come back when I can, Scarlett Bird."

She giggled. "I will be here."

No sooner had the door shut behind the sheriff than Marian rose from her place behind the chests.

"He is in love with you," she said needlessly.

Dulcina nodded. "Yes, he is. He has been for years." She peered at Marian. "That is why he killed my William, you know. Then I came here, where he keeps me safe."

Marian stepped forward. "This is not safe, Dulcina. It is a dungeon."

"Who can keep you safer in a dungeon than a sheriff?" The other woman asked. She held out her right hand, palm up. "And see? He made sure everyone knows I belong to him."

Marian gasped. On Dulcina's palm was a brand. It was unlike anything she'd ever seen; a series of circles, overlapping each other again and again until the pattern itself was almost lost.

"He *branded* you?" Her voice trembled. She reached out and gently took the woman's hand in one of hers, tracing the circles with one fingertip. The entire thing was raised, each circle a small line of puckered skin. Marian's eyes filled with tears.

"Why are you crying?" Dulcina's voice was soft and filled with curiosity.

"You do not understand," she sniffed. "He branded you."

"How else would he keep me safe?" Dulcina looked at Marian with wide brown eyes. "Who did you say you are?"

Marian shook her head. "I am sorry," she dropped Dulcina's hand. "I am afraid I wandered in here by mistake. I should leave."

"Come back soon. I love having visitors."

Marian fled without a backwards glance.

Chapter Twenty-Three:

Marian flew up the stone passageway and back to the light of the used portion of the castle. It was only when she reached the stairs leading back to her suite that she stopped running. A few servants glanced at her curiously and she realized how frightful she must look, with the dust of the dungeons clinging to her gown and hair. The faint sound of music came from the great hall but she ignored it and continued up the steps to her suite. She pulled the door open and slipped inside; praying Mother and Father were not there. She was correct. Not pausing, she continued into her rooms and collapsed on the bed. Before long, she was asleep.

"Marian," Mother's voice preceded the shaking of her shoulder. "Marian, it is time to get up."

Marian tried to open her eyes; they felt glued shut.

"You have slept through breakfast, and services, too." The bed creaked as Mother sat down. "I do not know what you did last night, but it is well past noon, and no-one likes a slug-a-bed."

Marian stretched and forced her eyes open. "I went down into the dungeons."

"Why would you do that?"

"The ghosts led me there." She sat up. "They wanted me to find someone."

"Who did they want you to find?" Mother asked.

"Dulcina Scarlett," Marian said. "It was Will's mother. The sheriff is in love with her, Mother."

The other woman stared at her. "That is an interesting development."

"There is more," Marian said. "She is completely mad, Mother. I do not know what he did to her, but she is not right in the head anymore."

"The Scarlett women never did handle stress well," Mother said absentmindedly. "But regardless, she cannot be left down there."

"Do you think Prince John knows?"

Mother shrugged. "It doesn't matter. Dulcina did not do anything wrong. Five years in a dungeon is a stiff price to pay for not loving someone back. Get changed and wash your face. There is someone we need to talk to."

Marian pushed back covers she did not remember pulling over herself. The light green gown she still wore was bunched uncomfortably under her and she tugged it down. "Who are we going to see?"

"The Lady Nyneve," Mother replied. "Hurry up. I shall wait for you in the sitting room."

As soon as Mother closed the door behind her, Marian changed into a clean white gown, laced it up and put on her shoes. "What do you think Nyneve will say?" She asked Mother, following her out of the suite and down the corridor.

"*Lady* Nyneve, Marian. She deserves your respect." Mother admonished her, but Marian could tell her heart was not really in it. "She has lived longer than either of us combined. If anyone will have any ideas on this—situation—it will be her. Our history always said she preferred the outdoors to anywhere else, so we shall try the gardens first."

Marian hurried to keep up with Mother's pace. "Why did not you tell me about her?"

Mother laughed. "When, exactly, Marian, would you have listened to me about anything? While I was busily acting like a featherbrained idiot, or when you were spending all your free time in the forest?"

"Father could have told me."

"He did," Mother's voice was mild. "He gave you the ballads. Did not you read them?"

Marian flushed. "I read some of them, but did not have time to finish them before we left," she said.

Mother nodded. "I understand, but you really should read them. Soon."

"I will." Marian promised.

They walked in silence until they reached the gardens.

"Why does she prefer the outdoors?" Marian asked.

"She is…who she is. Her power has always been in growth and greenery." Mother said. "I just hope she can help us."

"Help you with what, Lady Beatrix?" Nyneve startled them, stepping out of the brush as they walked by.

"We find ourselves with a very unique problem," Mother said, continuing to walk. Nyneve fell in beside Marian.

"If I remember correctly, you are more than capable of solving unique problems. I am not sure why you are coming to me."

Mother stopped in her tracks and turned to face the old woman. "Because you are The Lady of the Lake," she said bluntly.

"I have not been called that in hundreds of years," Nyneve returned. "But what is this problem of yours? Maybe I can offer some advice, if nothing else."

"I would appreciate that," Mother said. "But it is not my story to tell. It is Marian's."

"Let us have a seat, shall we?" Nyneve turned off the path and seated herself on a marble bench. "Now what did you have to tell me, children?"

Marian smothered a laugh at the idea of both her and Mother being called 'children', but she obeyed Nyneve's direction and took a seat next to the other woman. Mother sat down on the other side.

"I found someone in the dungeons who I want to get out," Marian said.

"You mean Dulcina Scarlett?" Nyeneve asked calmly.

"You—you know about her?" Marian gasped. "Why have you not done something?"

"And what would you have me do? Tell Prince John? Are you so sure he does not already know?"

"What game are you playing at?" Mother demanded. "Why would you leave her down there to be tortured by the sheriff? What kind of a monster are you?"

Thunder rumbled in the distance. Marian glanced up at the sky; it was clear and blue.

"What history knows of me," Nyneve said, "is a drop compared to everything I am. Never make the mistake of believing differently, Beatrix."

Mother glared back at her. "That woman in the dungeons is my *friend*, Nyneve. Do you even remember what friendship is?"

Nyneve sighed. "I cannot release her. The sheriff's feelings for her are...complex... and he would never stop searching for her if she escaped him." She shook her head. "There are certain factors in play that will help facilitate her release. In time."

"So what am I supposed to do now? Just forget I saw her?" Marian questioned, one hand curling a lock of her hair over and over.

"Yes. That is exactly what you need to do. I know it will not be easy, Marian, but it is the way it has to be. The ghosts will keep her company, and she them." She held up one hand to forestall Mother's statement. "Yes, Beatrix, I know what I am doing."

The Lady's voice was calm but Marian glanced skyward again and watched a lightning bolt arc out of the clear blue sky, sizzling down past the castle battlements.

Marian's jaw clenched. "She was branded, Lady Nyneve."

"She will heal." Nyneve said. She dusted off her impeccable white gown and rose to her feet. "This conversation is over."

"That...was not very helpful," Marian said, watching her walk away.

"On the contrary," Mother replied. "It was quite the opposite."

Marian narrowed her eyes. "How do you mean? She will not help us."

"We have someone else we need to contact." Mother rose. "Have you learned of the secret passageways yet?"

"Which passageways do you mean? The one at the back of the chapel or the one in the maze garden?"

"The garden would be easier," Mother said. "Come on, it is time to see Robin."

"What does he have to do with any of this?"

"We need him to kill the sheriff."

Chapter Twenty-Four:

"Kill the sheriff? What are you talking about?" Marian scurried after Mother.

"It is the only way to free Dulcina and keep the throne free for Richard's return." Mother explained.

"But—King Richard is in the Holy Land." She glanced at Mother's stern face as she hurried alongside her.

"I have heard rumors that tell me differently," she said. "I have no way of finding out how true they are, but even the possibility of their accuracy frightens me."

"What rumors? What are you talking about?"

"Austria," Mother said. "The last rumor I heard was that Richard had left the Holy Land and was taken prisoner while crossing Austria. If that is true, then I fear for his safety. Duke Leopold is not easily forgiving of insults, and I am afraid Richard has a volatile temper."

"I am not sure what that has to do with Robin," Marian said.

"Were you not listening? Pay closer attention. This is important, probably the most important thing which will happen in your entire life. We need to ensure the safety of the throne."

"Will the prince not notice when we kill his closest friend?"

"Of course he shall notice," Mother walked into the maze garden, the yew trees cool and inviting. "But the thing you do not understand about Prince John is this: he is ineffective at best. The sheriff is the true power behind the throne, Marian. Their relationship is like that of a chicken with its head. It functions well enough with it; eats, breeds, etc. But once the head is gone, all it does is run around the barnyard, waiting to fall."

It did not take long to reach the honeysuckle curtain guarding the entrance to the passageway.

"Watch your footing." Marian stepped down into the passageway. Mother dropped it behind her, enclosing them both in a blackness so complete Marian was sure she could see shapes where none existed.

"Did you ever use this in your days as a spy?" Marian's question was hushed.

"On occasion it was necessary." Mother replied.

Then came the unmistakable sound of flint striking stone. Mother suddenly appeared in front of her, holding a wildly sputtering torch in one hand.

"Where did you get that?" Marian asked.

"You would be surprised," Mother said, "at the number of items that can be hidden in a gown. I do not know how long the torchlight will last, so we had better hurry." She hastened up the passageway, the torch held in front of her like a beacon of hope.

Marian rushed after Mother. The hard packed dirt below her feet seemed to go on forever.

"How much further until we reach the end?" In the bobbing light, Marian could see nothing but Mother's dimly lit figure ahead of her.

"It is a long passage," Mother said.

"Surely it must end sometime!" Marian protested, the stitch in her side growing worse.

"It will when we reach Sherwood Forest," Mother answered.

Marian turned her head to look back down the hall. "Do you think—oof!"

"If you had not turned your head, you would have seen the door," Mother's voice was mild.

Marian rubbed her left cheekbone. "Ouch."

"Indeed," Mother said. She gently moved Marian out of the way. "Let me open the door first."

She placed her shoulder against the dirt encrusted door and pushed hard. It creaked open, the cobwebs in the corners tearing free and hanging to brush against her face as she stepped outside the narrow corridor.

Marian followed, breathing in the scent of damp leaves and letting it out slowly. She was home. "I missed this."

Mother nodded knowingly. "I understand. I always loved the way the forest smelled. I hated having to play the role I did for a lot of reasons, the least of which meant having to stay away from Sherwood." She smiled at Marian's astonishment.

"You both should visit the heart of the forest," Nyneve said. She floated over the grass to where Marian and Mother stood, her feet barely touching the ground.

"How—how did you get here so quickly?" Marian asked.

Nyneve winked. "This is *my* domain. Besides, it would take me a hundred years plus a hundred more to tell you all my secrets, and we do not have that kind of time. Beatrix, I am glad you understood my message."

"The implications were rather clear," Mother said sharply. "I am not a complete idiot."

Nyneve barked out a laugh. "I know exactly who the du Luc women are, and 'idiot' is not the word I would use for any of them. I do hope Robin is listening." Raising her head, she pursed her lips and whistled; three long notes and two short ones. "It should not take long, now."

It did not.

Robin was the first to arrive. He bowed elaborately to Nyneve. "You summoned me?"

The Lady's voice was solemn. "I did, Robin of Locksley. I have a task for you, and only you can accomplish it."

"Anything for you, Lady." Robin's tone was equally solemn. For an instant. He grinned. "But I claim a kiss as forfeit."

"You are cheeky, and some day that shall get you into trouble," Nyneve scolded, but her granite colored eyes twinkled.

"Well, luckily for me, you need my help," Robin teased the old woman.

"Are you going to say hello to your betrothed?" She laughed when Marian flushed red.

"I have not—" Robin started, but she shook her head.

"Do not bother denying it, Lord Locksley. You have had your heart set on her since she nearly bested you with Excalibur."

It was Mother's turn to gasp. "You dueled Robin with *Excalibur*?"

"You never told me what the blade was!" Marian snapped. "How was I supposed to know?"

"She has a point," Nyneve said. "You can hardly blame her for using the blade *you* gave her."

"I am not blaming her," Mother defended.

"Hmph." Nyneve replied. "Regardless, now is neither the time nor the place for such discussions. Robin, we need you to kill the sheriff."

Robin's eyebrows crawled into his hairline. "You mean The Sheriff of Nottingham?"

"No, The Sheriff of London," the Lady replied. "Of course we mean the Sheriff of Nottingham."

"But...why now?" Robin glanced at Marian, his jaw clenching at the sight of the bruise on her cheek. "Did he do that to you?"

Marian flushed red again. "No," she murmured, embarrassed. "I did it to myself."

A smile began to quirk the edges of Robin's mouth. "I assume that is a story you will share with me later?"

"I highly doubt it," Marian returned.

"While all this is utterly *fascinating*," Nyneve said, "it does not solve our problem. Now, will you do it?"

"I did not realize it was a request, but since you asked so kindly..." He winked.

"Damnit, Robin, this is serious!" Mother ground out.

"I am fully aware how serious this is. After all, it is not your head with a price on it." Robin said calmly. "If I choose to have a bit of fun while contemplating my next course of action, that has nothing to do with you."

"Children, arguing will gain us nothing. Beatrix, I need you to give me Excalibur." Nyneve said.

"It is Marian's sword now," Mother said.

"And yet it is still hidden in a chest in your rooms. I will expect you, and it, in my rooms no later than this evening." The old woman turned to Robin. "You and I need to speak privately."

Robin bowed his head. "Can I have a word with Marian first?"

"You can have two." Nyneve said. She turned to Mother. "Come, Beatrix, let us allow them their privacy." Mother refused to move and Nyneve continued. "Either you trust them or you do not."

Mother sighed, but followed the Lady.

Marian stared at Robin through the dappled sunlight, the open door of the Sherwood passageway at her back. "Are you really going to murder the sheriff?" Her voice was low.

"It was not my first choice, but I trust Nyneve's judgment. If she thinks it is necessary, then yes. I will."

Marian swallowed hard. "He is an evil man," she whispered. "But...murder?"

"Tuck tells me the ghosts like you. Did they tell you it was the sheriff who actually placed the nooses around their necks and pulled them tight?"

She shook her head.

"He has a great deal to answer for, Marian." Robin smiled somewhat grimly. "But I do not want to talk to you about that now. I have missed you. Have you been well?"

"Considering where I am, yes. But I miss the forest," she sighed. "The gardens are lovely, but walking in them is not the same. It is an artificial loveliness."

"You will be home soon enough," Robin promised, touching her bruised cheek gently. "We will be together sooner than you think."

"Marian, it is time for you to return with your mother." Nyneve interrupted them. "I am sorry I cannot give you longer together, but we have much to accomplish and not a lot of time."

Marian smiled at Robin. "I trust you," she said.

He pressed a kiss against her palm and folded her hand over it. "Be safe."

"Good grief," Nyneve grabbed Robin's hand and hauled him through the trees, leaving Marian and Mother alone in the small clearing.

Chapter Twenty-Five:

"What now?" Marian turned to Mother.

"Now we go back to the castle before we are missed," Mother said.

"And do what? Pretend we have not been planning anything? I do not think I can do that."

Mother placed one hand on each of Marian's cheeks, cradling her head. "Listen to me carefully, Marian. You have no other choice. If you do not play your part, and play it well, we will all be hanged as traitors." She softened her voice. "I have lived this for years, Mari. You will be fine as long as you remember to breathe. Now, are you ready?"

Marian took a deep breath and released it before nodding. "Yes, I think so."

"Good girl." Mother walked toward the passageway back to the castle. "I am proud of you, Mari."

"I—you are?"

"Yes, of course." She bent down, picked up the torch and cradled it under her arm as she struck flint to stone. Once the torch was lit, she continued. "My greatest fear has been of you turning out like one of those ladies you have met at court. And yes, I see the irony, considering you thought me one of them for years. But I could not tell you about working with Robin. I needed you to find out for yourself."

Marian nodded, following the bobbing light in front of her. "I wish you could have told me, but I understand why you did not."

Mother stopped suddenly. "Wait here, Mari. And be very quiet. Someone is outside."

The curtain parted unexpectedly.

"Lady Beatrix, thank God I found you!" Friar Tuck said. "The prince has guards combing the grounds, searching for you. You are to meet him in the throne room at once. You, and Lady Marian, of course."

"He wants us? But why?" Marian followed Mother into the maze.

"The prince would not lower himself to tell me," Tuck said, "even if I had an audience with him, which I did not. One of the guards thought I may know where Marian went, since she is known to spend quite a bit of time in the chapel."

"If Prince John wishes to see us, then we must go immediately," Mother stated calmly. "Whatever he has to say, he is our prince and we owe him our allegiance."

The woman who had spoken so frankly to Marian in the passageway and the forest was gone under a layer of court veneer.

"Will—will the sheriff be there?" Marian asked.

"Naturally, he *is* the prince's right hand man." Tuck escorted them through the maze and into the gardens, where they were met by three of the prince's personal guards.

"Lady Beatrix, Lady Marian, Prince John awaits your presence in the throne room. He sent us to ensure you arrive there in a timely manner."

Mother straightened her shoulders, and Marian followed suit. "We are honored to have you escort us."

The guards bowed their heads briefly. "If you are quite ready…"

"Yes, of course."

A light drizzle began to fall as they crossed the cobblestones to the castle. Marian could not help it; she glanced upward at the sky. Gray clouds stared back at her and she smiled. Unlike the thunder and lightning of earlier, this rain was natural.

The throne room was the biggest room Marian had ever seen. Tapestries of every hue hung on three of the four walls. The wall behind the throne itself was festooned with weapons; ancient swords, battleaxes and shields of every size. Prince John leaned back on the massive throne, looking like nothing more than a boy playing with his father's toys.

Father sat on multi-colored velvet cushions at the prince's feet, strumming idly on his lute.

"We are glad you could join us," Prince John said, his fingers steepled in front of him. "Lady Marian, I fear we shall have to postpone our duel. We have other concerns we must occupy ourselves with."

Mother and Marian sank into deep curtsies. "Your Highness," Mother murmured.

"We have been considering ways in which the du Luc House can best serve the throne," the prince said. "And we have come up with a solution we are well pleased with."

"Indeed, Your Highness?" Mother prompted.

Prince John leaned forward. "A marriage between my closest friend and your daughter would benefit both our houses."

The lute twanged at the same moment Marian gasped. Only Mother kept her composure.

"That is—most generous of you," she began. "But Marian is still young to consider marriage, Your Highness, and the sheriff is nearly twice her age."

The prince waved his hand. "That is of no importance," he said.

"And what does the sheriff think of this?" Mother continued. "Does he wish to marry a child?"

"It is of no account!" Prince John roared. "*I* am the ruler here!" He slammed his hand against the throne's armrest.

Father rose to his feet. "Your Highness, if I may speak?"

The prince visibly reigned in his temper. "What is it?"

"I would not see my daughter unhappy for the world, so I hope you understand that I would rather have this engagement postponed for a time, so they can get to know each other better. I understand it is rather unconventional, but your word here is law."

Marian's eyes flickered between Father, Mother and Prince John. "Your Highness?" She ventured. "I am new to court, and to court protocols. Unless I learned more, I do not think I would be an asset to you or to—to the sheriff."

Prince John arched an eyebrow at her. "You are forward, Lady Marian, to speak so to us, but we will forgive your lack of manners." He drummed his fingers on his velvet clad thigh. "Your engagement to Roger de Lacy will be announced tonight, and you *will* be married by Harvest time." His eyes flicked up and down Marian. "Make sure you are dressed appropriately. You would be unwise to disgrace our court with less than perfection."

Mother drew in breath to speak, but Father put a hand on her arm and she subsided.

"You are dismissed," the prince said. "The guards will see you back to your suites."

Mother, Marian noticed, did not curtsy again, but only tilted her head slightly. "Yes, Your Highness." Her submissive attitude did not change until they reached their rooms and the doors were shut and bolted behind them.

Chapter Twenty-Six:

Mother paced across the sitting room, her movements crisp and angry. "He *dares* engage Marian to that—that lunatic?? Without our consent? Alan, this is madness!"

"And what would you have us do about it?" Father asked mildly. "Until Richard returns, we are subject to his whims."

"We are going to kill him," Marian said.

Father stared at her. "Kill who? Prince John?"

"No, the sheriff," Marian exclaimed. "Did Mother not tell you?"

Father shook his head. "What's she talking about, Bea?" Mother sighed. "The Lady of the Lake wants Robin to kill the sheriff using Marian's sword. I was going to tell you *privately*, but there was no time."

"Unless she plans on it happening tonight, it does not solve our immediate problem," he said.

"I cannot be betrothed to the sheriff," Marian said. "How can the prince betroth me to someone without my permission?"

"He is our regent," Mother said. Her voice was bitter. "He can do anything he pleases. But do not concern yourself, Mari. You will never marry the sheriff. I will not allow it, even if I have to kill the man myself."

"I doubt it will come to murder," Father interjected. "The wedding will not take place until the Harvest. That gives us six months."

"And in the meantime what am I supposed to do?"

"For the interim, you will be a young, nervous bride-to-be." Mother said. "I still have to get Excalibur to Nyneve tonight, before the prince's announcement. Go down to the kitchens and see if Anna can rustle up a meal we can eat here."

"She has been spending a great deal of time there," Marian said. "I have hardly seen her."

"Anna has been occupied with one of the older pages," Father said. He shrugged when Mother raised an eyebrow at him. "The cooks are the backbone of every home, castles included."

"Regardless of her desires, her duties are here. Tell her to come upstairs at once."

"Yes, Mother," Marian said obediently.

Anna was not in the kitchens.

"No, milady, she has not been 'ere all day," one of the serving girls said, her hands full of assorted cheese wheels. "Last I saw 'er, she was with the sheriff's page."

Marian frowned. "Do you by chance know what they were doing?"

The girl shrugged. "Talkin', milady."

Marian narrowed her eyes. "I would never ask you to betray her, but is there any way you would know what they were discussing?"

"I do not eavesdrop, but I *did* over hear somethin' curious." She adjusted the cheese wheels in her arms. "They was talkin' about some special sword. Anna told him she knew all 'bout it."

"Thank you," Marian whispered, her voice suddenly gone at the thought of Anna having betrayed them all.

The serving girl ducked her head.

Marian stumbled out of the kitchens, her head spinning.

"Lady Marian, just the woman I was looking for," The smarmy voice of the sheriff met her. "The prince just informed me we are to wed. What an utterly delightful prospect." His tone implied marriage to him would be anything but.

"I—yes, that is what I was told earlier."

"Then I think a walk together would not be amiss." He took her arm. "Come, we have much to discuss before tonight's banquet." He propelled her at a brisk pace past the throne room and the dining hall.

"Sheriff, where are you taking me?" Marian tried to pull free of him but his grasp was unyielding.

"Somewhere we can have the privacy we need."

"I do not think—" Marian began, but the sheriff cut her off.

"Your thoughts are not my concern," he ground out. "You are my betrothed, sanctioned by the throne itself. Your only duty is to obey me."

"I think not!" Marian protested. "If this is the way you hope to endear yourself to me, allow me to inform you that you are severely mistaken."

"No, *Lady* Marian, you are the one who is mistaken." The sheriff continued past the stairs to Marian's rooms and down the old stone corridor. "You see, I know what you have in your possession. And I aim to have it."

"I have no idea what you mean," Marian said.

"Then please allow me to be perfectly clear," the man sneered, all semblance of courtliness vanished now that they were in the older part of the castle. "Your maid was most forthcoming with Phillipe. It was quite easy to gain the information we sought." He twisted her arm brutally, and she cried out.

"Stop it! Where are we going?"

"These doors, my *beloved*, are the dungeons."

"Wh—what? Why?" Marian writhed wildly in his grasp.

The sheriff pulled open a familiar door and tossed her inside, slamming the door behind them. "I have questions. And you *will* answer them."

Marian scrambled away from him. "I do not know what you want from me!"

He stalked closer. "Answers, Marian. I am not a fool. I know your family history."

"You brought me a visitor," Dulcina sang out unexpectedly. "Can I meet her?"

"Not now, Scarlett Bird," the sheriff growled.

"Ohhhh, you are angry." Dulcina cowered back in her chains. "But I have been good. I promise."

"I am not angry at you, Bird." The sheriff snatched at Marian's arm and hauled her up. "But I do not like liars, and your new roommate is a liar."

"You are mad if you think I am staying here," Marian snapped. Her foot shot out and she kicked him in the shin.

He grunted, but did not loosen his grip. "Lady Marian, it seems you are not a lady, after all. Very well, I shall treat you accordingly."

"You mean like you treated Dulcina?" As soon as the words left her mouth, Marian realized she had made a crucial mistake.

"It appears you have availed yourself of my dungeons before." His eyes narrowed.

Her back stiffened. "I have," she admitted. "And if the way you treated Dulcina is the way you treat women in your care, I refuse to be counted among them."

He dragged her to the wall opposite Dulcina. "Understand this. You do not have a choice in the matter."

She spit in his face.

The sheriff grabbed her by the throat.

Dulcina screamed. "Stop, stop it, you will kill her!!"

He released Marian's throat immediately. She began coughing.

"*He will not stop until you tell him the truth.*" The ghosts whispered. "*He wants the sword. It is the only way he can rule England. He needs it.*"

Marian shook her head. "But I do not know where it is."

The sheriff's eyes narrowed. "Who are you speaking to? It is those thrice damned ghosts, is it not??"

Cackling laughter rang out. The sheriff blanched.

"*He is scared of us.*" The teasing voices turned sober. "*He should be.*"

"Lady Marian," he hoisted her up and shoved her against the wall before chaining her legs. "Prince John has presented me with a unique opportunity, and I plan to take full advantage of it."

Marian looked up at him with tear streaked cheeks. "I will not marry you."

He laughed. "I have no interest in marrying you, and the beauty of my plan is that I will not have to."

"Are you going to kill me?"

"Of course not." He actually looked shocked at the idea. "No, you will remain here and keep Dulcina company."

"I shall be missed," Marian sank to the ground, her fingers already picking at the metal cuff around her left ankle.

A half smile played around the sheriff's lips. "Yes, you will; by your betrothed as well as everyone else in the castle."

"And where will you tell them I am?"

"Sherwood Forest, of course. You have been kidnapped by Hood and held for ransom. As your betrothed, it falls upon me to rescue you and ensure your safety."

"Ro—that would never happen!" Marian held her breath, hoping he did not notice the slip of Robin's name.

"It does not matter," the sheriff said. "As soon as I leave here, whatever I say will be the truth. Now, make yourself comfortable and think about where your family has hidden that sword."

"But what about afterward?" Marian could not help but ask. "Will you keep me down here forever?"

"That is not a possibility," he said. "Your mother is a descendant of the crown. She will not rest until you are found."

It was Marian's turn to look smug. "Then it appears as though you have a problem."

The sheriff shrugged. "Once my plans come to fruition, any problems I may have will be easily solved."

He glanced over at Dulcina, still cowering in her own set of manacles. "Everything will be all right, little Bird. Do not fret."

"Then—then you are not angry anymore?" She queried.

He shook his head. "Not at you, never at you." He smiled. "I love your new dress."

The other woman grinned. "'Is it not pretty? The maid who brought it said you gave it to me." The chains about her ankles clinked when she rose to her feet. "See?" Dulcina held her arms out. Elaborate floor length sleeves brushed the stone flooring of the dungeon.

"It looks beautiful on you," he said.

"Will you dance with me?" Dulcina tilted her head to one side.

"I wish I could, Scarlett Bird," the sheriff returned. "But I have court business to attend to first."

The older woman pouted. "But then you shall come back and dance?"

"If I can, I will. I promise." He blew her a kiss before striding across the room and shutting the door behind him.

Chapter Twenty-Seven:

"He will come back," Dulcina swept her arms back and forth, watching the blue wool sleeves drag on the floor with a rapt expression. "If he leaves the torches lit, he always comes back." She giggled.

"Do you remember me?" Marian asked.

Dulcina frowned. "You look familiar. Do I know you?"

"I am Will's friend; Beatrix du Luc's daughter."

The other woman shook her head. "You cannot be Marian. Why, you must be nearly grown! Marian is but a child, nearly a year younger than my Will."

"Will is seventeen," Marian said. "And I turned sixteen last month."

"That is impossible." Dulcina said flatly.

"It has been five years," Marian insisted. "Will was just barely thirteen when you were brought here."

"Why would I come here? This is not my home."

Marian bit back a sigh of frustration. "You came to the castle after your husband was murdered to claim justice for him. You never returned."

"But Will is all right?" Dulcina sat, her feet curled underneath her.

"Yes, of course he is. He was raised by your sister, Constance." Marian bit her lip, unsure of how much she should tell the other woman.

"I had a sister once," Dulcina said dreamily. "Her name was Constance." She leaned forward, peering through the torchlight at Marian. "Is she still alive?"

Marian nodded. "Yes, her and Will live in a house very close to us."

"That must be nice. Will always needs more friends. He is such a lonely boy."

It was, Marian realized, going to be difficult to get Dulcina to understand what had happened to her. She sighed and tried again.

"Do the ghosts speak to you often?"

Dulcina smiled, and it lit her entire face. "Oh, yes. They are wonderful company."

"What do they speak to you about?"

"They tell me stories," she said, "about their lives here. It sounded like great fun."

Marian frowned briefly. "Do they ever tell you why they died?"

"No, we do not speak of such things. They are—" she shrugged. "Uninteresting."

"What are their names?"

"I have no idea. It seemed unimportant." Dulcina raised one eyebrow. "Do you need me to ask them for you?"

"No, I have spoken to them myself." Marian said.

"All you had to do was ask," the shadows said. *"The eldest is Dalen, and his brother is Alair."*

"Then why are you bothering me with such questions?" Dulcina yawned suddenly. "I am tired. Can you come and visit me tomorrow?"

"I fear you will have my company for a time," Marian returned.

"Oh, good. I love having company stay the night." The other woman smiled at her sleepily. "Good night...what did you say your name was?" Without waiting for a reply, she curled into a ball, her head resting on her arms.

"Marian," she said softly, not knowing if Will's mother would remember when she woke up. "My name is Marian."

"Are you lonely? We can keep you company while she sleeps," The shadows crawled up the dungeon walls until all the stones were black.

Tears trickled down Marian's cheeks. "I am not lonely," she admitted. "I am scared."

"Prince John will not harm you," they said. *"Not like he did us."*

145

"No one knows why you were killed; only that the sheriff and the prince did it." She sniffed. "What if they decide to condemn me to the same fate?"

"The sheriff was correct. He cannot afford to harm you."

"Because he wants Excalibur," Marian stated.

"What he wants, he will not get. But that does not mean he will not bring you grief."

"What do you mean?"

"He is adept at pretense, and you are confined."

"Why do you sound more like the Lady of the Lake, and less like children?" Marian narrowed her eyes suspiciously.

"Very good. I can, upon occasion, use the boys for my own purposes." The Lady sounded amused. *"Now listen carefully. Even now, the castle guards are readying themselves to tear Sherwood apart, searching for you."*

"Who is coming to rescue us?" Marian could not disguise the eagerness in her voice.

"No-one," Nyneve replied. *"At least not immediately. I am sorry, Marian, but your fate dictates that it is not I who shall be the instrument of your release."*

Marian glanced at where Dulcina slept. "It hardly seems fair."

"Nevertheless, it is necessary. Be patient. Help will come."

"When?" Marian asked.

"When what?" The voices were the voices of small children once more.

Marian leaned back against the wall and closed her eyes. "Never mind," she whispered.

Chapter Twenty-Eight:

"Time to break your fast!" The announcement was followed by the opening of the dungeon door.

Marian opened her eyes blearily. At some point during the long night, she had fallen asleep, curled into a ball. She tried to stretch her legs and cried out at the cramping pain that shot through them.

"If you rub them, it will help." Dulcina sounded surprisingly lucid.

"Thank you. Umm…do you know who I am?" Marian obeyed the other woman's instruction, carefully stretching out first one leg, then the other.

Dulcina smiled and Marian's heart leapt with possibility.

"She does not." The guard pushed the door shut behind him with the thrust of one meaty hip. "I brought enough food for both of you. If you," he addressed Marian, "are agreeable, I have permission to allow you to eat together. If not, you can eat whatever she may toss your way."

Marian looked him over. He was a large man; not as large as Little John, but imposing in his own right and the sword he carried had obviously seen use. "I agree."

"A guest!" Dulcina clapped her hands merrily. "It will be a feast!"

The guard placed two trays on the floor next to Dulcina and strode toward Marian.

"The sheriff told me what you did," the man said. "If you spit upon me, I will eviscerate you, royal background or no. Do we have an understanding?"

Marian gulped. "We do." She sat quietly while the guard unchained her legs.

"Can you stand, or do you need help?" He asked, one hand dropped to his sword.

"I can stand, but I cannot walk," Marian said. She rose to her feet and accepted the hand he held out. Little fissures of a needle like pain raced up both calves, but she gritted her teeth and hobbled across the floor to where Dulcina still sat.

"I shall come back this evening," the guard said. "I have the sheriff's betrothed to find and a substantial reward to collect." He winked at Marian. "Did you know the sheriff is offering a king's ransom for your safe return?"

"I—how can you do this?" Marian asked, shifting from one leg to the other in a vain attempt to regain all feeling in them.

"He promised me a certain position at court once he has the throne." The man shrugged. "Bein' a guard has its perks, but it is not what I want." He yanked the door open. "Do not attempt anything." The door shut behind him.

"I do not know what he expects me to try," Marian muttered, more to herself than anyone else.

"He wishes to be the court torturer." Dulcina handed Marian a crisp pastry. "There, try that."

Marian obediently bit into it and warm strawberry filling filled her mouth. "This is delicious."

"These are my wedding samples," the other woman said. She smiled and Marian saw the beginnings of a dimple. "William wishes me to try everything on the plate. I think he secretly wishes me to gain weight before we wed!"

"William...you mean Will's father?"

Dulcina frowned. "I have had no children outside the marriage bed! What sort of light woman do you take me for?"

"I did not mean to offend you." Marian took another bite of the pastry and chewed thoughtfully. "Where do you believe we are?"

"Home," Dulcina popped a piece of cheese into her mouth. "Where else would I be?"

"Do you think she understands?" The shadows began whispering. *"She cannot be healed."*

"So what would you have me do?" Marian licked her fingers free of strawberries. "Stop trying? Are you not the ones who led me down here to begin with?"

"We cannot remain here forever," they retorted. *"The prince is in attendance and we have things to do. She needed the company."*

"Besides," a single childish voice said, *"they are coming and they like you."*

That was all the warning she received before the two ghosts from the battlements formed in front of her. Alair's lips curved in a smile.

"More company!" Dulcina sang out. "If you are cold, boys, take a torch from the wall. I am sorry I have no fire. I have not seen a maid in some time and I seem to have mislaid the fireplace."

Marian blinked. Dalen and Alair laughed silently.

It felt rude to eat in front of them, but her hunger outweighed her manners and she grabbed another pastry. This one was filled with cheese and spices.

"Which ones do you like best?" Dulcina asked eagerly. "I do not wish to disappoint William with my choices."

"Everything is delicious. Do you eat this way every morning?"

"Oh, no. Only when company comes," the other woman replied.

"Has there been much company since you arrived?" Marian picked up a goblet and took a small sip. It was as she feared. Honey mead.

"A few visitors, but none stayed long. They must have had nightmares, because I heard them screaming during the night, but when I would rise for breakfast, they would already be gone."

Marian shuddered. No wonder the woman was mad. The boys floated over to Marian and sat themselves next to her, folding transparent legs underneath their bodies. They sighed.

"I wish I could share the meal with you," Marian told them.

Alair reached out and gently touched the back of his hand to Marian's cheek. She gasped at the feeling of rough silk dragging across her flesh, and he smiled again.

"They are precious," Dulcina said. "I wish I had children."

"You do," Marian said a trifle sadly.

"Who are your parents, dear? I cannot imagine them allowing you to stay out so late."

Marian wanted to scream. "No, ma'am, they do not. But I informed them you were hosting me tonight and they said it would be all right."

Dulcina's smile was childlike in its simplicity. "Oh, good. I did not want to remain here alone."

"Soon we will both leave this place," Marian promised. "The boys promised me."

"They are good boys," Dulcina said. "If they say we are going to leave, then I should pack my things." She began to gather the food on the tray into a pile.

"Do not concern yourself with it," Marian said. "I will ensure your things go with us when we leave."

"*She is getting better at communicating with her,*" the shadows said happily.

The brothers nodded their agreement.

"*I will miss them when they leave,*" said the lone boy who had spoken to Marian before.

"Are you sure we cannot leave with them?"

Dalen and Alair nodded again.

All the shadows sighed in disappointment.

"You mean you cannot leave the castle? Ever?" Marian asked.

The ghosts shook their heads in unison.

"*They are coming for you, Marian. Be ready.*" Once more, the words belonged not to the murdered children, but to the Lady of the Lake.

"Who is coming for me?" Marian asked, but even as she watched, the shadows crawled down the dungeon walls, across the room and oozed underneath the door, leaving her and Dulcina alone with the only two ghosts in the whole castle who lacked the power of speech.

Chapter Twenty-Nine:

"Are you leaving already?" Dulcina asked. "Would you like me to make you up a basket?"

"*We* are leaving," Marian corrected.

"I hope it is in a carriage," she said. "I have always loved carriage rides."

"We might ride in a carriage afterward."

"Will the sheriff be joining us?" She tilted her head to one side. "I like him. He takes care of me."

"No," Marian told her. "He cannot come with us on this trip. It would not be appropriate." It was the best answer she could think of.

Alair floated over to Dulcina, resting his head on her shoulder. She smiled. "He is the sweetest child. Do you think they would like to come with us?"

"I am positive they would, but they have to stay here," Marian replied. She was about to say more, but was distracted by the lock on the door being turned.

Dalen and Alair vanished abruptly.

Two hooded figures rushed inside, drawn swords held in clenched fists.

Dulcina began to shriek. "Go away! We are waiting on a carriage, go away, go away, go away!!" She lowered her head to her knees, hands held over her ears.

The two men, for Marian could tell at a glance they were men, slammed their shoulders against the door. It flew shut and the one closest to it twisted the lock.

"Dulcina, Dulcina, shhh…" Marian knelt at the other woman's side. "Look, look, they are not hurting us, they are simply here to…" her voice trailed off, and she looked up at the men. "Who are you and why *are* you here?"

"We are here t—to resc—cue you." Lord Aelfred said, throwing back his hood.

Marian blinked in surprise. "Aelfred, how on earth did you find me…us?"

The second man threw his own cowl back. Familiar gray eyes smiled at her. "Why, Maid Marian, did you think I would refuse the opportunity to rescue you myself?"

Her heart tripped at his voice. "Robin," she smiled in relief. "But…"

"It was the Lady," Robin said. "She sent word to me and I slipped in through the front gates. Apparently the betrothed of the sheriff warrants a massive search party. Now, may I kidnap you in truth?"

"I will not leave Dulcina behind," Marian stated.

"I would never dream of it." Robin turned to the man at his side. "Lord Aelfred, if you would be so kind."

"Of c—course," he stuttered. He sheathed his blade and knelt down. "Lady Dulcina, my name is Aelfred. C—can you lower your hands and listen t—to me?"

Dulcina sat up slowly. "Are you going to take me in a carriage?"

Aelfred glanced at Marian, who nodded. "Of c—course," he said. "If that is your wish. But in order for us t—to leave, we need t—to be as quiet as possible. C—can you do that for us?"

Dulcina nodded happily. "It is akin to a game of hide and seek, then?" She reached up for the hand Aelfred extended to her and slowly rose to her feet, the chains around her ankles clanking together.

The red-haired courtier smiled. "Yes, it is something like that."

Robin narrowed his eyes. "Aelfred, can you pick a lock?"

Aelfred snorted his amusement. "It was never a sk—kill required at c—court."

"Well then, I shall have to do the best I can." Robin bent down, pulling a slim strip of metal from his waistband. "Now, if I remember how to do this…" He inserted the metal into the right manacle and jimmied the clasp open.

Marian gasped. The flesh around Dulcina's ankle was raw and oozed a whitish clear liquid.

"Do you think she can walk?" Marian whispered to Robin.

He turned to the other ankle and in two flicks of his wrist, that manacle came loose as well. "It does not matter." His answer was brutal in its honesty. "If she cannot walk, then she must be carried. Every available guard is descending upon Sherwood Forest with the hope of collecting the reward the sheriff has posted."

"Is it so very much, then?" Marian's curiosity got the better of her.

Robin barked a laugh. "It rivals the bounty placed on my head," he admitted. "Whatever value the sheriff sees in you is great."

"C—can I help you?" Aelfred questioned Dulcina.

The other woman shook her head. "I do not understand what happened to me," she said, her voice high and frightened. "Why do my ankles hurt so much?"

"You have not used them without the manacles in many years," Robin said softly. He touched the other woman's shoulder. "But if you allow it, Lord Aelfred can help you."

"He said he would take me in a carriage. Are you sure he was telling the truth?"

"I was not lying," Aelfred said. "If you leave with us, I promise you will ride in the grandest carriage at my disposal."

Dulcina bit her lip. "Is it drawn by a set of matching horses?" She struggled to her feet, wincing as her ankles bore the support of her body without the added weight of the chains.

The tall red-head smiled gently. "I have a pair of beautiful grays and I would love t—to show them t—to you, but it is important that we leave immediately."

"Oh, all right." She took a single step forward, but her ankle folded underneath her and she would have fallen if Aelfred had not caught her in his arms.

"Place your arms about my neck, and I will c—carry you," Aelfred said.

Dulcina smiled at him flirtatiously. "This is most improper, but since we are to be wed, I will allow it." She wound her arms around him and laid her head against his chest.

Aelfred flushed and Marian saw Robin smile as he bent down to help her to her own feet. "Most of the guards have left the castle," he said. "But we still need to be careful. I will go first. Aelfred, Marian will take your sword and guard the rear."

Aelfred threw a glance at Marian. "Are you sure that is wise?"

Robin smirked. "She is better than most men with a blade," he said. "I would trust her with my life, and you would be wise to do the same."

The older man nodded. "I do not wish t—to put Dulcina down. You may t—take my sword."

Marian bit her lip, but removed Aelfred's sword from its sheath. Robin unbolted the door and the four of them slipped into the empty corridor.

Chapter Thirty:

"The passageway has been cleared," Robin stated, "but it will not stay that way for long. We need to get to the chapel."

"Where is the sheriff?" Marian asked.

"He left for Sherwood Forest after informing your parents of the 'kidnapping'." Robin said.

Marian could only imagine Mother's reaction to that. "Mother did not say anything—"

"She was quite distraught, as you c—can well imagine." Aelfred said. "Then she sent for me and told me to bring the Lady Nyneve t— to her. The historian is a force t—to be reckoned with. She informed me I was t—to go int—to the forest and find Robin of Locksley. I had no int—tention of doing so, but then I found myself exactly there, doing exactly that." His voice was wondering.

"You have no idea," Marian muttered under her breath.

"Keep your head lowered when we reach the more populated areas of the castle," Robin instructed. "We will not be out of danger until we reach Sherwood." He belatedly pulled his cowl back up and Aelfred followed suit.

They hurried down the corridor, the dust from the floor rising into their nostrils. Marian stifled a sneeze as they emerged from the dim passageway and into the castle proper.

"Friar, you startled me!" A serving girl squeaked at the sight of Robin. Then she saw Dulcina in Aelfred's arms. "Oh, do you need me to summon a surgeon? Is she all right?"

"She is well enough," Aelfred said, walking forward until he blocked her view of Robin and Marian. "I was walking with her and she fainted unexpectedly. I am taking her up t—to her—her rooms."

The girl's eyes widened and she blushed. "Her rooms? Oh, yes, milord." She scampered off.

Robin quirked an eyebrow at Aelfred's back. "You are taking her to her rooms? Do you realize that girl will spread the gossip far and wide?"

Aelfred shrugged as best as he could with the silent Dulcina in his arms. "I had t—to say something."

"We are to be married," Dulcina said. "A soft bed would not be amiss."

"I c—could never do that," Aelfred said. "It would c—compromise you unbearably."

Dulcina unwound one arm from his neck and patted his cheek. "You are sweet," she said. "Are we going to your carriage?"

"As soon as we c—can, my dear," Aelfred said. "I promise."

Robin strode past Aelfred and Marian. "The castle is deserted, if we move quickly we should be able to reach the chapel without incident."

It didn't take them long to reach the chapel doors. Robin pulled them open and gestured Aelfred and Marian inside, bolting the doors shut once they had entered.

"Why are we here?" Aelfred set Dulcina down gently in a pew. "I do not see how this will help Dulcina."

"We are waiting for someone," Robin said. "Once he arrives, we can leave."

"Leave and go where?" Aelfred demanded. "I will not put Dulcina through the st—tress of hiding in the friars quarters."

The door at the back of the chapel swung open and Tuck walked through it, straightening his robes. "The forest is overrun with guards," he greeted them. "Nyneve wants to know if you can travel unseen to the heart."

Robin shook his head. "I cannot, not with Dulcina's injuries."

Tuck frowned. "Then we will travel as best we can for as long as we can. Lord Aelfred, I can take Dulcina from here. Your part in this need not continue."

The red-haired man gazed down at Dulcina, who was swaying gently in her seat, her eyes closed and a half smile upon her lips. "I would prefer t—to st—tay with her," he said. "She needs me right now."

"You are a good man, Aelfred. I am sorry Prince John never saw your value."

"If he had, I c—couldn't have helped him." He pointed to Robin. "Or Dulcina."

"Is it time to go?" Dulcina glanced up at the sound of her name.

"Yes, it apparently is." Aelfred lifted her and she snuggled close to him again.

"Marian, your parents are eager to see you again," Tuck said. "Allowing you to remain in the dungeons was—difficult—for them."

"I can imagine," Marian said. She began to hand Aelfred his sword, then paused. "Uh, do you want this back?"

"My arms are full," Aelfred said, "and it appears you c—can handle one just fine."

"It is not the same as Ex—as mine, but it is well balanced."

"Enough chatter," Robin said. "Tuck, we will follow you."

It did not take them long to reach the end of the chapel corridor and open the door.

"I must return to the chapel," Tuck said. "I will meet you later." He pushed the door and as it slid shut Marian could see him trotting back up the dark expanse.

"About damn time you arrived," Nyneve stood, arms crossed, at the edge of the small clearing.

"My Lady, I am heartbroken at making you wait," Robin said with a grin.

"Step aside, Robin, and let me see to Dulcina. Things are progressing more rapidly than we had anticipated. The sheriff is approaching the heart of Sherwood."

"You are allowing that?" Robin sounded surprised.

Aelfred spoke from behind Robin. "How is it up to a hist—torian t—to allow anyone int—to Sherwood? I thought the forest was the king's domain."

Maybe it was the trick of the light, but Marian was positive the historian became taller and somehow more regal in the white tunic and leggings of soft doeskin.

"The heart of the forest has always belonged to me, Lord Aelfred." Nyneve's granite colored eyes glowed eerily in the reduced light of the forest. "Come, children. Dulcina needs help and we have a man to murder."

"Wait, what?" Aelfred protested. "I did not agree t—to murder anyone!"

"It is not up to you," Nyneve said. "And it will not be done by your hand." She pointed at Robin. "He will do it with Excalibur."

Chapter Thirty-One:

Robin raised one eyebrow. "For someone intent on keeping that blade secret, you are suddenly quite unconcerned about who is listening."

"Aelfred will not say anything about it," the Lady said blithely. "Once we reach the heart, he will understand."

"But how can we reach the heart if the heart is in us?" Dulcina mused.

"The sheriff has a great deal to pay for." Nyneve said grimly. She walked through the grasses, the blades growing thick and lush around her ankles, some daring blades even reaching up to clutch at her calves as she passed by.

Aelfred paled and his arms tightened involuntarily about Dulcina. "Do the plants here normally behave that way?"

"They like me," Nyneve said shortly. "Quickly. We do not have much time left before he arrives."

"Is he hunting Robin because of me?" Marian asked, breathless.

"It is not that simple," Nyneve replied. "The kidnapping scheme was but an excuse to do what the prince has been denying him permission to do since Richard left."

"I thought Prince John *wanted* Hood brought to just—tice," Aelfred stuttered.

"He does, but John refused to give him permission to actively hunt Robin," the Lady said. "With Marian's kidnapping, that ban was lifted." She stopped suddenly and raised one hand. "Quick, into the trees!"

They scrambled to obey her, the urgency of her voice spurring them on.

"Clear the path," a deep voice stated.

"This is the king's domain," Nyneve stated calmly, "and I do not believe you are here on his business."

"We are here on the sheriff's business," the voice answered.

"Which is not the same as the king's," the Lady replied.

"The sheriff charged us to find his bride and return her safely to him."

Nyneve snorted her amusement. "Is that what he told you she was?"

"Why are we listenin' to her?" A different voice asked. "She be nothing more than the historian."

"Wrong," Nyneve snapped. Thunder rumbled.

The men glanced up. "The sky was clear when we started..." one of the men said nervously.

"It is the beginnings of a thunderstorm, nothing else," the first voice replied.

"I heard about what lives in the deep woods. If we search, will we be allowed to leave?"

"Why would you ask me?" Nyneve sounded amused. "According to your man there, I am only the castle historian."

Marian felt something touch her ankle and stifled a squeal. It was the fronds of a giant fern, caressing her in a way that was wholly unnatural for a plant. Robin reached out and gave her hand a reassuring squeeze.

"The villagers say you be something else."

"King Richard allows me the use of this forest, and all its paths. If you wish to search, I will not stop you, for that is your right. But it is my right to refuse to...how did you put it?...'clear the path.'"

"Come on, we can find another way," the nervous man said.

"I will tell the sheriff of your disobedience," the first man stated.

"Tell the sheriff *this!*" Nyneve snapped and Marian felt the air grow heavy seconds before a flash of lightning nearly blinded her.

"The sheriff can search for her himself!" One of the men cried out. "No woman is worth bein' struck!" Heavy boots retreated the way they had come.

"You can come out now." The Lady's voice was calm.

"What in all the hells was *that*?" Aelfred was the first to emerge from the tree line, his arms empty.

"Where is Dulcina?" Nyneve demanded, not answering his question.

"I c—could not hold her indefinitely," Aelfred said. "She is braiding grass int—to rings." He shrugged at the Lady's surprised look. "It k--kept her occupied and quiet. Now, will you t—tell me what happened?"

"I sent the sheriff's guards away with a message," she said.

Robin's mouth quirked to one side as he stared at the lightning struck tree. "That was quite a message."

The Lady shrugged. "They annoyed me, and it bought us a bit of time. Aelfred, if you would collect Dulcina, we can be on our way. We are scant feet from the heart."

"You will hardly keep your identity a secret if you flaunt your power." Robin still held Marian's hand in his and he tugged her forward to stand by his side.

"Richard already knows who I am, as did his father before him." Nyneve started along the path once more, the overhanging trees pulling their branches away as she passed underneath.

"And I am unconcerned with either the sheriff, who will be dead shortly, or John, who should be more concerned with Richard's return than wild tales told by a handful of cowardly guards."

The path ended and the Lady turned to them. "Wait here until I come get you. I cannot guarantee your safety otherwise."

Marian turned to Robin. "What does she mean by 'guarantee your safety'?"

Robin shrugged, but there was a small smile tugging at his mouth.

"If you do not wish to tell me, then just say so." Marian tried to tug her hand free of his, but he refused to let go.

"That is not it, Marian," he said. "But the forest holds secrets that are not mine to tell and the heart is the nexus of Sherwood."

"Aelfred, bring Dulcina in," Nyneve's voice carried through the tangle of underbrush and trees in front of them.

"And us, Lady Nyneve?" Robin asked. "Are we welcomed, as well?" Marian began to walk forward. "No, Mari, wait. It is not safe yet."

"Yes, you two may enter as well." Nyneve stated. "Your parents are here and eager to see you."

Tears welled up in Marian's eyes at the thought of seeing Mother and Father again. "Oh yes!" This time Robin released her hand when she pulled it free. She hurried forward, entering the underbrush behind Aelfred and Dulcina who were directed by Lady Nyneve deeper into the heart.

Marian's immediate impression of the clearing was dulled by seeing Mother and Father, rising to their feet from their seats on a large stone.

"Mother!" Marian rushed into Mother's open arms.

"I am so happy to see you!" Mother stroked Marian's golden, tangled, curls. "Are you well? Did he hurt you?"

Marian shook her head. "Yes and no. He did not hurt me, but I do not know what might have happened if Robin and Aelfred had not arrived."

"We owe them a great debt of gratitude," Father said, "that can never be repaid."

"This might not be the best time," Robin said, "but I cannot think of a better one, considering our circumstances. Alan, Beatrix, would you do me the honor of giving me Marian's hand in marriage?"

Chapter Thirty-Two:

"Wait, what?!" Marian pushed free of Mother's arms. "I think you forgot something, *Lord* Locksley!"

"No, I do not believe I have," Robin said. "You do love me, do you not?"

"I—I," Marian stuttered. "What do I say?" She appealed to Mother and Father.

"Do not ask me," Mother replied. "It is not my proposal. I am already wed."

Father just shook his head, his lips twitching.

"It is not *my* proposal, either!" Marian snapped. "If you love me as you claim, then ask me, not them."

"I was but observing proprieties," Robin protested, but his eyes were sparkling gleefully.

"You are jesting with me," Marian said, her heart falling unexpectedly at the thought.

Robin immediately sobered. "I thought to lighten the mood with my approach," he admitted, "but I was not jesting. If you will have me, Marian du Luc, it would be my honor and privilege to marry you, after I kill the sheriff."

It was not quite the proposal she had dreamt of but, Marian's lips quirked into an unwilling smile, it was Robin.

"Does that smile mean you will?" Robin asked.

"I will consider it," Marian returned tartly, though her heart was singing.

Mother turned to Father. "I suppose you have something further to say before you collect on your bet?"

"What did you bet on?" Marian glanced at Father, who refused to meet her eyes.

"Me??" She gasped. "You bet on something to do with *me*?"

"Not precisely," Mother said. "It was more on Robin than you."

Robin began laughing. "I cannot believe you would do such a thing!"

Marian looked at all three of them. "What am I not understanding?"

"Sweet Mari, you parents bet on us." Robin explained. "I am assuming you, Alan, bet on my winning your daughter's hand while you, Beatrix, bet against it."

"I did not bet against it, merely the timing of it." Mother said, laughter bubbling up in her throat at the look on Marian's face.

"It was a wager made in fun," Father said. He leaned toward Mother and planted a quick kiss on her lips. "There. Payment rendered."

"I cannot believe you are Mother," Marian said. "How did you fool me all those years?"

Mother shrugged. "I have had years of practice pretending to be something I am not."

"So now you have been reduced to wagering on your daughter's happiness?" The Lady floated through the opposing underbrush, barely touching the grass of the clearing, which strained up to meet the soles of her feet. Marian's worn leather belt was wrapped about her waist.

"I will take a harmless bet where I can," Mother said calmly. "Is Dulcina settled?"

"Yes, she is with Aelfred and resting comfortably." Nyneve said. "Robin, are you ready to meet the sheriff?"

"Is he just waiting for me?" Robin asked.

"No, but he *is* searching close by." She unbuckled the belt holding Excalibur and held it out to Robin. "You will need this."

He took the blade with reverent hands. "Are you sure—" he began.

Nyneve smiled. "Some fights cannot be won at a distance. Excalibur will help you, Robin. Trust it."

"Robin, what if he kills you?" Marian spoke softly.

"It is Excalibur, Marian." Robin said. "I am sure it will protect me as well as it did King Arthur."

Marian's brow crinkled. "But he was defeated."

Nyneve floated between them. "Children, there is no time for this. Beatrix, Alan, will you stay here and keep an eye on Aelfred and Dulcina?"

Mother and Father nodded in unison.

"I will be fine, Marian." He took her hand in his and kissed it. "Remain here and I will return as soon as I can."

Marianshook her head. "No, I will not remain behind while you face him alone."

"Lady, I will not allow her to come with us!" Robin declared.

"*You* will not allow? Robin of Locksley, you forget your place," Nyneve bit out. The forest darkened briefly around them. "*She* is not facing anyone. You are. But if I know anything about your lady, she will not wait idly by while you are gone. Therefore, she will come with us now, and save me the trouble of finding her later."

"I will not argue with you, Lady," Robin said. "I know as well as any villager whose forest this truly is."

Marian turned to Mother and Father. "I will come back."

Father had his arms wrapped around Mother. "We know." He nodded at her. "We will talk when you return."

Marian followed Nyneve and Robin, being careful to stay camouflaged among the green leaves of the giant ferns and tall grasses. Huge oaks seemed to bend their trunks out of the way when Nyneve strode past and Marian could hear what sounded like whispering at the very edges of her consciousness. She opened her mouth, but before she could say anything, Nyneve held up one wrinkled hand. "Wait. He's through those ferns, Robin." Nyneve's voice was hardly more than a whisper. "Focus on the sheriff. Once you defeat him, the others will fall."

"Marian," Robin faced her. "If I asked you to stay here, would you?"

She smiled and shook her head. "You know me better than that."

"Yes, I do." He pressed a kiss to her forehead. "At least watch from behind the trees, then. Will you agree to that?"

Marian nodded and stepped with him as he pushed his way through the massive ferns. She hugged the tree trunk close and carefully peered around it while he continued forward.

Chapter Thirty-Three:

The sheriff rose from his knees at the sound of Robin pushing through the brush. He had, Marian noticed, managed to start a tiny fire, which sparked and sputtered angrily.

"Well, well, I did not think Hood would find me before I found him," the sheriff said. One hand smoothed immaculate hair away from his face.

"And I did not think to find you alone, with nothing more than a—" Robin cocked one eyebrow at the struggling flames, "what *would* you call that?"

"A fire," the sheriff said flatly, "and I never said I was alone."

Robin raised an eyebrow at the sight of the six men fanning out behind the sheriff. "I always thought you were a coward. I see you have chosen to confirm my beliefs."

The sheriff clenched his teeth so hard Marian could hear them grinding against each other. "On the contrary," he bit out. "I simply see no point in soiling my hands with your traitorous blood."

"I am no traitor," Robin retorted. "Refusing to bow down to an untried prince and his toady is not traitorous, it is merely common sense."

"You know," the sheriff drew his sword. "I put a bounty on your head hoping someone else would find you, but it will be much more satisfying to kill you myself before rescuing my betrothed from your clutches."

"She is not your betrothed," Robin scoffed. "She would no more marry you than I would!"

One of the guards snickered. The sheriff turned and, in one fluid movement, ran the hapless man through. As he dropped to the ground, Marian bit back a gasp.

"If you continue to kill everyone who laughs at you, soon there will be no-one left," Robin taunted.

"Kill him," the sheriff said flatly. "The reward is doubled!"

There was the *snick* of five swords leaving their sheaths, but Robin was not done yet.

"Are you too afraid to come after me yourself?" He stepped backward, weaving Excalibur back and forth.

"Wait," the sheriff ordered harshly. "I shall do it. No man will call me coward and live." A few of the men frowned, but he waved his free hand. "Oh, do not worry. You shall still be paid for your services. Prince John will reward us *all* greatly when I bring back Hood's head." Without warning, the sheriff's blade snaked out, thrusting at Robin. Excalibur, crackling with eerie blue sparks Marian had never seen before, easily swatted the attempt aside. The sheriff's eyes narrowed. Robin grinned ferociously.

"That is quite a blade you have," the sheriff said. "I do not believe I have ever seen its like." He thrust again, and again his sword was parried by the blue sparking blade. "I might be persuaded to spare your life to own such a sword."

"I am not ready to give this blade up," Robin said. With a twist of his wrist, Excalibur struck out with incredible swiftness, shedding more blue sparks in its wake. "You see, it was a wedding gift from the Maid Marian."

Marian gasped, but neither man heard it.

The sheriff laughed. "I sincerely doubt that since she is enjoying my hospitality at this very moment."

"You mean the hospitality of the dungeons where you imprisoned her, along with Dulcina Scarlett?" Robin winked. "Suffice it to say, sheriff, I have taken *both* your prizes."

"NO!" With a cry of outrage, the other man thrust his sword at Robin.

Robin danced lightly backward. "They were happy to come with me and escape you," he said.

"You lie," the sheriff hissed. "Dulcina would never voluntarily leave me."

"Your Scarlett Bird has flown its nest," Robin smirked. He lunged forward, but his foot slipped in the wet grass. The sword flew from his grasp.

"No!" Marian dove out of the concealing trees, her hand outstretched. She scrabbled in the leaves, praying she would make contact with the pommel of Excalibur.

"Quick, grab her!" The sheriff snapped at the men still milling about. "What are you waiting for??"

Marian's hand touched the arming sword and she pushed it in Robin's direction even as rough hands grabbed her shoulders and yanked her upright.

"Be careful, you clods! That is my betrothed!" The sheriff said.

Marian spat out bits of grass. "I will *never* marry you!"

"You will not have a choice," he retorted. A slow smile crossed his face and he stalked closer. Marian shrank back in the guard's grip. "Once I depose the prince, there will be nothing stopping me."

"Nothing except King Richard," Robin said. "And me." He lifted Excalibur out of the leaves. "And this."

"I hardly see an absent king, an outlaw and an ancient, though curious, sword as a threat to be taken seriously."

"That is your mistake," Robin said. In a move like water pouring from a cup, Excalibur swung out, slicing a thin line across the arm of the guard holding Marian captive. She pulled loose and scrambled to stand behind Robin. "You will never have the Lady Marian," Robin continued. "Nor Dulcina."

"Dulcina is mine," the sheriff said. "She will always be mine." He lunged forward, blade outstretched.

Excalibur met his sword with a resounding clash and a shower of blue sparks that had Marian shielding her eyes.

"What the—" the sheriff fell back and Excalibur, with Robin holding the hilt, followed him with a flurry of whip like blows. The sheriff dropped his sword as he raised his hands to shield his face. Robin thrust and Excalibur came to rest, point pressed up against the other man's chest hard enough to draw blood.

Chapter Thirty-Four:

"Why not kill me immediately?" The sheriff panted. "You disarmed me; there is no reason for you to wait."

"I do not need to prove my worth by killing you," Robin said contemptuously. "However, killing you for Dulcina's sake would be my pleasure."

"I never harmed her. I kept her safe; I love her."

Marian eyed the guards watching them. They shifted from foot to foot without meeting her steady gaze. "I saw what you did to her," she finally said. "You branded her. What sort of a man does that?"

The guards shook their heads. "It is not right," one of them muttered. "I will be no party to murder." The others nodded in agreement.

"Cowards!" The sheriff spat. "Then be gone with you! I will deal with this outlaw on my own!"

"Hand him his sword, Mari," Robin commanded. "I will not murder a helpless man."

"Your nobility will get you killed." The other man promised. He accepted the blade from Marian, drawing it across her palm in the process.

"Oww!" Her hand welled with blood.

Robin's eyes went flat. "That is the very last courtesy I will do you," he said. Excalibur seemed to agree, its point pressing deeper against the sheriff's chest, leaving a spot of blood against his white shirt.

The sheriff flinched and stepped farther back. "I believe you promised me a fair duel," he said.

Robin brought Excalibur up to his face in a salute before striking out. Blue sparks rained down, but this time the sheriff was ready for the light and struck through it. Marian gasped when Robin barely deflected the blow.

"Help him," Marian pleaded with the guards.

"No, milady, this is not our fight." One of them said.

"Then leave," she snapped. "Run back to the castle like the vermin you have proven yourselves to be!"

The guards all looked at each other, then back at where the sheriff and Robin fought, blades sparking and clashing in a continuous bout. "If we take *her* back to the castle," one murmured, "we can still collect the bounty from Prince John."

Marian's eyes widened. "No, can you not see? I have not been kidnapped, I am not being held here against my will. What will taking me back to the castle accomplish?"

"My mum is a villager," one guard said. "I became a guard to work for the throne, not for a man who tortures women and holds them hostage against their will."

The first man spoke again. "Well, I could use the monies the sheriff promised us."

"Do you really believe he will pay us? Or even survive?" The second man questioned.

Marian glanced away from them and toward Robin.

Excalibur shed sparks as it beat relentlessly against the other blade. The two men thrust and parried their way across the clearing.

"I think either one of them could win," the first guard said. "I would prefer to have my payment, and I am sure Hood will not be the one to offer it."

"I will not go with you willingly," Marian stated. "And Prince John will hear the truth of the matter; that you have brought me to him against my will. What do you think he will do to you then?"

The men looked at each other uneasily.

"You *could*," Marian suggested, "take the sheriff back instead. After all, he was the one who kidnapped me, not Rob—Hood. I am sure the—the prince would reward you handsomely for your service."

"We could do that," the first guard said. He shrugged at the other men's incredulous looks. "I do not care where the money comes from, so long as it comes. But keep a grasp on her, just in case."

The second guard nodded and moved to Marian's side. She shifted slightly to the left, but kept her eyes glued to the scene taking place in front of her.

"What do you think John will do to your band of outlaws," The sheriff parried a blow from Excalibur, "if you succeed in killing me?"

Robin struck again. "The prince has never concerned himself with the outlaws of Sherwood. That has always been your personal vendetta, not his. And now you wish to lay claim to the throne itself?"

"John," the sheriff panted, "is not man enough for the throne. England needs a firm hand."

"England has one," Robin retorted. Excalibur began to glow a steady blue as Robin forced the sheriff further and further back toward a huge, towering oak, its branches heavy with moss and mistletoe. "Richard rules here."

"Richard rules nowhere!" The sheriff screamed. "The king is not coming back! *I* will be the ruling power here!"

Excalibur's glow increased until the whole clearing was bathed in light. "I think the sword disagrees," Robin said.

"A sword does not have the ability to agree or disagree," the other man gasped, his back pressing against the tree trunk.

Robin smiled, sweat beading his brow. "This one does."

"Wait," the sheriff said. "I have heard rumors of a sentient blade—a blade nearly older than time... I know that sword! Prince John would give all the riches of the throne to own it!" The blade nearly leapt out of Robin's hand, thrusting deep into the other man's chest. In a leap of logic only the dying are allowed, he solved the sword's mystery. "It's Excal—" The blade twisted a final time, piercing his heart and forever silencing the word on his lips.

Chapter Thirty-Five:

The clearing fell silent as the sheriff slid off Excalibur to lie, slumped, at Robin's feet.

The five guards standing close to Marian stepped away and shuffled their feet while he cleaned the now quiescent sword and sheathed it.

"It was the money," one of them finally spoke, his voice low. "We would not have harmed her, but we needed the reward."

Robin nodded. "I understand the lure of gold as well as any other man. Go back to the castle. I have no quarrel with you."

"You are not what the sheriff claimed," the first man said. "We will stand at your side for what happened here." He glanced at the two bodies on the clearing floor before motioning to the rest of his men. They obediently followed him out of the clearing.

"Well done, Robin," Nyneve said, her face wreathed in smiles as she floated through the trees, the bottoms of her feet barely touching the patches of moss vying for space with the lush grass.

"I am glad that was done to your satisfaction," Robin said, but his eyes were on Marian.

She walked toward him, careful not to stare at the body near his feet. "Robin." Her eyes welled with tears.

His mouth tilted up in a rakish grin. "I told you I would be fine."

The tears began rolling down her cheeks. "I—I know," she sniffed. "But—Oh, Robin, that was close!"

"If you lovebirds are *quite* done, I would like my sword back." Nyneve spoke. "Oh, and you will want to take care of those." She pointed to the bodies on the ground, nostrils flaring. "Have them buried below the oak. It could use the fertilizer."

"But—Prince John—will he not miss the sheriff?" Marian began.

"The prince has more pressing matters to deal with than the death of his 'friend'." Nyneve said. "Soon he will have to answer for everything he has done."

As though to emphasize her statement, trumpets sounded from Nottingham Castle.

Robin raised an eyebrow. "Why the royal trumpets? The prince is already at the cas—" his voice trailed off.

"It is the king," Marian breathed. Her heart started pounding.

Robin whirled to stare at the Lady, who smiled serenely. "Is it true? Has King Richard finally returned?"

Nyneve ignored the question. "Marian, we need to return to the heart. Your parents will be worried. Robin, take care of the bodies, please."

"But Nyneve, are the trumpets for Richard?" Robin persisted, one hand lingering on the sword at his waist.

The Lady stared pointedly at Robin's hand. "You will want to remove your hand before you cause an accident."

Robin flushed. "I would never—" he began, but she cut him off.

"I know that, but Excalibur might not." Her voice was utterly devoid of humor. "That sword was forged to my specifications in the realm of Avalon. You may wish to treat it with more respect."

Robin immediately fumbled for the buckle holding the sheath to his waist and undid the clasp. He held it out. "Thank you for the loan, then, but I do not believe I need it any longer."

The Lady of the Lake took Excalibur back and buckled it about her own waist in one swift movement. "Now that the sheriff is dead, I can return Excalibur to its resting place."

"Are you telling us Robin could not have defeated him on his own?" Marian asked, twining one hand with Robin's.

"I was trained with a blade while growing up," Robin said, "but I was an indifferent student at best. I much preferred the longbow."

"If Excalibur cannot tolerate evil, then why has someone not killed the prince with it?" Marian questioned.

"Prince John is not pure evil. In fact, he is not evil at all; just inattentive and misguided. With Richard's return, he will pay a price for the deeds he has committed, both against England and against the innocents he murdered." Nyneve swiftly plaited her long hair so it hung in a thick white braid past her waist. "Robin, if you would take care of the bodies before they begin to stink…"

Robin pursed his lips. Two shrieking whistles pierced the forest, one following the other in rapid succession.

The tangle of Klamath Weed, Field Rose and Meadowsweet bent forward as Little John pushed through them, followed by a very young boy Marian had never seen before.

"Whatcha--" the big man's eyes dropped to the sheriff's body. "Oh, I see. Caused a bit of a mess, did ya?"

"It is good to see you, John." Robin released Marian's hand and stepped forward to clasp the hand Little John held out. "I would say I cleaned up a mess rather than caused one."

Little John grinned. "Two bodies seems a bit of a mess to me." He shrugged. "You need help disposing of them?"

"I need them buried by the oak," Robin said. "Much, you have your knives?"

The boy nodded. There was an air of barely restrained violence in the way he held himself. Marian shivered.

"Who is that?"

"Much the Miller's son," Robin replied. "He is a good kid provided you do not attempt to part him from his blades."

"I would not dare," Marian murmured. She took Robin's hand back in hers. It felt safer.

The young boy grinned, as though he knew exactly why she did it. "What you need, Robin?" He raised one knife to his mouth, biting idly on the flat blade.

"Once Little John buries the bodies, carve a warning into the oak," Robin instructed. He grinned. "Make it a memorable one."

"Understand this, however," Nyneve pinned Much with a stone colored glare. "If you carve too deeply and injure the tree, no knives in the world will spare you from my wrath."

A flicker of fear crossed the boy's face. "No, Lady. I would not 'arm the tree for nothin'."

Nyneve nodded smugly. "See that you do not. Come, Robin, Marian. Let us collect your parents and be on our way." Without waiting to see if they obeyed, she left the clearing.

Robin and Marian stared at each other for a long moment before Robin broke the silence. "Little John, keep an eye on Much." He turned to the boy. "Much, behave. No killing *anything* without Little John's permission. Understood?"

The boy looked rebellious, but nodded.

With a last backward glance at Much, Marian followed Robin out of the clearing.

Chapter Thirty-Six:

"Marian, I am so happy you are safe." Mother said. Father pulled her to her feet and they both rushed forward.

Marian released Robin's hand and stumbled forward, into their embrace. "The guards wanted to take me back to the castle to collect the reward and Robin killed the sheriff and then Little John came to bury the bodies..." her voice trailed off.

Father smoothed Marian's hair over and over. "It is over, Mari. You are safe now."

"We need to return to the castle," Nyneve said. "Beatrix, I want you with us. Alan, you may come if you wish, but it is not required."

"We heard the trumpets," Mother said. "I am looking forward to seeing Richard again."

"I will not leave my daughter," Father stated.

"I did not expect you to." Without a backward glance, the old woman marched out of the clearing. "Robin," she called over her shoulder, "you need to come with us."

"She is just as bossy as she ever was," Mother muttered under her breath.

"And she is old enough that she is unlikely to change," Father retorted. "So we may as well do as she demands."

"Instead of complaining about me," The Lady's voice carried through the underbrush, "you may wish to catch up. I will not wait forever."

Marian snickered. She took Mother's hand in one of hers and Father's in the other.

"Are you in love with Robin?" Mother's voice was lowered so Robin, striding ahead of them, could not hear.

"I—think so," Marian said. "I do not know him very well, but I could be."

"He is a good man, as was his father before him." Father said.

Marian's eyes widened. "Are you both giving me your blessing?"

"According to Robin, you are already betrothed, so do our blessings matter?"

"I did not accept him yet," Marian said. "And the idea of marriage is terrifying."

"Then you are not ready," Father said. "Robin will understand that."

Marian bit her lip. "Do you think so? I would not hurt him for the world."

"It is not a decision you have to make today, regardless of what he said before the duel with the sheriff." Mother reassured. "Richard is back and we can return home soon." She smiled. "There is no doubt in my mind that Robin will allow you the time you need. After all, he is still an outlaw, and now a murderer as well. He will be required to plead his case before the throne to ensure he does not spend the remainder of his life in Richard's dungeons."

"Do you believe the king would do that?" Marian stared at Robin's broad back as they continued through the forest.

"The king has always had a fiery temper," Mother said. "A great deal will depend upon his mood."

"But he cannot possibly think punishing Robin for killing a madman is just!" Marian protested.

"Marian, he has to weigh the facts, must act as the magistrate from town does to in order to determine a fair outcome," Father said.

"I cannot see the fairness in sending him to the dungeons for doing a service for the throne!"

"Prince John will have a chance to speak about the sheriff's actions, Marian. Do not concern yourself overly with this." Father squeezed her hand. "It is but a formality. Richard will not allow harm to come to innocents; even innocents driven to ill deeds."

"Marian," Robin stopped walking within sight of the castle portcullis, and turned around. "I trust the king, and so should you. Whatever comes, I will accept his judgment as one based on what is best for the kingdom."

Marian was silent, staring at the raised iron gates. Soldiers milled around in uniforms brown with dust.

"Where is the Lady Nyneve?" Mother asked. "Is she at the castle already?"

Robin nodded. "Yes, she said she would fetch Richard and bring him to us."

"Can she do that?" Marian's eyes were wide. "Just order him to come?"

Mother shrugged. Her hands smoothed down the gray silk gown she wore. "She can try, but the Lionheart does not take orders lightly."

Father's rich baritone disagreed. "The king is not a fool. He will listen to her." His hazel eyes sparkled. "Imagine, Bea, the ballads I could write if she would speak to me of her part in the legends of Camelot."

"She was only mildly involved in that whole mess," Mother said. "Nyneve may have put the wheels in motion, but the true tale would have to come from Merlin, or Arthur himself, which is impossible."

"I suspect the Lady had a heavier hand in the matter than she wishes anyone to believe," Father said.

"Ask her about it once this is over." Mother shook her head, smiling. "But do not blame me if she tells you nothing. She has not lived over five hundred years in secrecy by telling tales of any kind." She focused past Marian's shoulder and her eyes widened.

Chapter Thirty-Seven:

One of the tallest men Marian had ever seen strode toward them, followed by Nyneve, who had changed into an ornate gown of flowing white silk. The man's face was strong, with a square jaw and flame colored curly hair worn cropped close to his head.

"Richard," Mother breathed, sinking into a low curtsey. Father bowed low, as did Robin.

"Marian, down," Mother hissed, tugging on Marian's sleeve.

Marian sank to the ground, bedraggled skirts spread out around her. She raised her head and watched the king approach. His leather armor was covered in dust and the only distinctive marking she could see was a gold ring on his smallest finger.

"Richard, this is why I summoned you." Nyneve said. "I believe you remember Lady Beatrix du Luc and her husband, Alan a Dale."

"Beatrix," King Richard rumbled, "it is good to see you again." He raised Mother to her feet and kissed both her cheeks. "You are most welcomed back to my court. And Alan, it has been far too long since I had the pleasure of hearing your lute."

"Thank you, Your Majesty."

"Do you remember Robin of Locksley?" Nyneve asked. "His father served you well."

"Of course I remember him," Richard said warmly. He turned to Robin, one eyebrow raised. "You look—earthy."

Robin grinned. "I have spent a great deal of time in the forest as of late," he admitted.

"We shall have to discuss why. I am sure there is an interesting story behind it." Richard turned to where Marian still curtsied. "And who is this charming girl?"

"This," Robin helped Marian to her feet, "is my betrothed, Marian du Luc."

"I have not agreed to marry him yet," Marian responded tartly, belatedly adding, "Your Majesty."

"It seems you have a difference of opinion on your hands, Robin." Richard said.

"She is opinionated, Your Majesty, but then again, look at her parents." Robin winked.

Richard roared with laughter. "I might be careful of my words, if I were you," he said. "Beatrix is not one to trifle with."

"Indeed not," Mother said briskly. "Richard, did Nyneve tell you anything of what has been happening in your absence?"

"All the Lady told me was that it was important we speak, and speak in private." He grinned, the shadows under his eyes vanishing temporarily. "We have no better opportunity than here and now."

"Why did you leave the throne to John, Richard?" Mother asked bluntly. "Did you really see him as the best choice?"

"What are you saying, Beatrix? He was the *only* choice."

"Well, he made a mess of things," Mother said. "He put the sheriff in charge of everything, not just Nottingham."

Richard's deep gray eyes darkened. "You have been invaluable to the throne, but be careful of what you say. He *is* my brother."

"Did you know he outlawed good men for no other reason than their loyalty to you?" Mother continued. "Robin is proof of that. John killed Lord Locksley and declared both him and his entire house, traitors to the throne. As a result of that accusation, Robin has spent the last five years living in Sherwood."

Richard turned to Robin. "Is that an accurate assessment??"

"It is, Your Majesty."

"Tell me all of it," Richard commanded.

Robin began with the tale of his father's death and continued up to Marian's supposed kidnapping.

Richard frowned when he finished. "That is a fantastic tale. Where is the sheriff now, to answer your charges?"

"I killed him," Robin admitted.

"That is *not* the answer I hoped to hear, Robin." Richard's storm cloud eyes turned almost black. "Care to explain to me why you murdered a man of my court?"

"He *branded* a woman." Marian chimed in. "Robin did not murder him. It was a fair duel."

The king swung to face her and Marian shrank back under his glare. "*Murder* is what I call it until it is proven differently, and that is unacceptable in my court, Lady Marian."

"Richard, if I may speak?" Mother waited until he nodded before continuing. "The sheriff kidnapped my daughter and attempted to lay the crime at an innocent man's feet. If that is not a cause for action, I do not know what would be."

"I am not denying action needed to take place, Beatrix. But needless murder is not something I will ever condone, not after what I have seen in the Holy City."

"What about the ghosts, Your Majesty?" Marian's voice was small and barely audible.

Richard frowned. "What ghosts are you referring to? My castle has never been haunted!"

"I was not sure how to tell you," Robin said, shifting from foot to foot.

"Tell me everything' means I wish to know everything," Richard said. "I have shown great restraint, but if you do not tell me what I need to know, you will spend the rest of your days praying desperately for my favor. Do I make myself perfectly clear?"

Robin swallowed. "Yes, Your Majesty, but I think it would come best from Marian. She has had more experience with them than I have."

Richard cocked an eyebrow. "Is that true, Lady Marian?"

Marian nodded. "Yes, Your Majesty." She took a deep breath and released it slowly. "Though, in truth, I am unsure where to begin."

"Begin with the ghosts," Richard commanded. "Do you mean to tell me my castle is infested with spirits?"

"Infested might be too strong a word," Marian said at the very same moment she heard Robin say, "Infested' is the perfect word."

Richard looked around the clearing, finally choosing to seat himself on a fallen log. "What happened?"

"No-one is exactly sure, Your Majesty," Marian began.

"John ordered the murder of dozens of children and the sheriff carried it out," Father said. "If anyone deserved to be killed, it was that man."

"My brother murdered children??" Richard's voice was incredulous.

"After you left," Mother said, "many nobles, both here at court and in Wales, protested against your brother's arbitrary judgments and ham-handed rulings. He responded by demanding they send him their sons as hostages."

Richard nodded. "That has been a time honored tradition to prevent rebellion. I am not surprised my brother did so. But you claim he murdered them? Why would he do such a thing?"

"No-one knows, Your Majesty," Marian said. "All I ever knew about was rumors. At least, that is all I knew until I came here and met them."

Richard blinked. "Did you just say you met them?"

Marian nodded. "Yes, Your Majesty. Most of them appear as shadows, when they appear at all. But they apparently enjoy playing pranks, especially when the prince is in residence." The king crossed his arms across his barrel-like chest. "Well, to the Devil we sprang and to the Devil we shall go! It seems my brother and I have much to discuss. He has not been a worthy example of a ruler, to allow such a monstrous thing to happen."

"Your Majesty, if you do not mind my asking…where have you been these last few years?" Mother asked. "I heard a rumor of Austria. Was it true?"

Richard nodded. "I am afraid it was. The last dispatch I received from England informed me of John's deceit. I chose not to believe the dispatch, though I planned to return home on the next available ship. Unfortunately for me, I shipwrecked along the coastline of Italy and was taken hostage by Duke Leopold shortly thereafter." He sighed. "John ignored my imprisonment for nearly twelve months. He sent word instead that the coffers were empty and he needed more time. I realize now why it took him so long to ransom me." He rose to his feet and clapped his hands together once. "Well then, it is time to return to the castle and set my kingdom back to rights."

"Would you like us to wait here?" Robin asked.

The king shook his head. "No, you all have first-hand knowledge of what has transpired in my absence. I will require your presence when I speak with John."

"Meet me in the throne room," Richard glanced briefly at Robin. "I shall send an armed escort for you. I do not want you killed 'accidentally'."

Robin bowed. "Thank you, Your Majesty." His voice was devoid of any sarcasm.

The king nodded once before striding off, his long legs eating up the ground.

"I see Richard has not changed much," Mother said drily.

Father nodded his agreement. "I am glad he is back. England needs him."

Marian turned to Robin. "Do you believe he will pardon you?"

Robin grinned. "I hope so. I cannot provide for my bride without a pardon for my crimes."

"I already *told* you," Marian said, "I am not marrying you."

"You protest too much," Robin stated.

"I would not have to protest if you would stop calling me your bride!" Marian replied shortly.

The steady tramping of boots on the ground stopped further conversation.

"Those must be the guards," Mother said. "I do wish the Lady had not taken Excalibur so soon," she said under her breath. "I always felt better with it by my side."

Eight guardsmen dressed in well worn leathers approached. "We have instructions to bring you to the castle at once," the first one said. He glanced curiously at Robin.

"Thank you," Mother's voice was low and honeyed. She took Father's arm. "We appreciate your thoughtfulness."

The man nodded curtly, gesturing at his men to form a protective circle. "Not that we expect any trouble," he explained, "but the king made it very clear you were to arrive unharmed."

Marian looked past the guardsmen toward the castle. It appeared to be only a field's distance away.

"Then let us go," Mother said. "I would not wish to keep King Richard waiting."

Chapter Thirty-Eight:

"His Majesty will see you now." The guard at the throne room door gestured and pulled the doors shut once they entered.

Marian expected to see the king seated on his throne. Instead, he was sprawled across the steps leading up to the ornate chair. He had changed from the leather armor and into a dark blue doublet and leggings. A thin gold circlet sat on his red hair. He looked every inch a king.

A door behind the throne itself swung open and Nyneve, so steeped in shadow ghosts that her white gown appeared to undulate an inky blackness, stepped into the room.

"We are here," she said, "to see justice done." The shadows eddied and swirled, never leaving her clothing.

Marian shivered.

Richard nodded to Nyneve and Marian got the impression he was acknowledging the ghosts' presence, as well. "I will not fail you, or them," he promised. "Alan, Beatrix, stand with Nyneve. Robin, you and Marian join them."

The enormous ornate doors to the throne room opened and four guards entered. Marching between them, pale and shaken, was Prince John.

"John." Richard walked the few feet separating him from his brother. He reached out and pulled him close. "It is good to be home."

The prince stood stiff in his brother's embrace. Finally, reluctantly, he patted Richard on the back. "I am glad you have returned safely, brother."

The king stepped away. "Unfortunately, this cannot be a simple homecoming. There are things which must be resolved. First of all, do you remember this man?" He pointed to Robin.

"I recall seeing him at court some years ago," the prince said. "But I have not seen him in some time. I thought the Locksley household moved away."

"I find that fascinating, considering it was your orders which consigned him to the life of an outlaw." Richard said.

"I—did what??" Prince John's eyes widened. "I did no such thing!"

"It was your signature on the orders," Richard said. "As the regent to *my* throne, it was your responsibility to surround yourself with good and trustworthy men, instead of signing any random piece of parchment thrust beneath your nose." He began to pace the marble floor. "Instead, you put your childhood friend in the position to wreak utter havoc in my absence!"

"I did not know," the prince began to protest, but Richard cut him off with a wave of one large hand.

"I shall assume, for the moment, that you are simply too trusting." His voice lowered. "Care to explain something else to me, John?"

"Richard, I swear I did not know. I thought his family left court," the other man shrank backward.

"I am not referring to what the sheriff did to the Locksley household," Richard said, "but to what happened on the battlements."

Prince John blanched. "N—nothing happened."

"Wrong," Richard said flatly. "You murdered children, John."

"Rumor," the prince said. "That is pure conjecture."

"It is the truth!" Richard roared, his voice echoing off the high ceiling. "Not rumor, not conjecture! It is the truth!"

The prince turned, as though to leave, but the guards stepped close.

"There is no escaping this, John." The king's voice dropped low and deadly. He glanced at Nyneve before continuing. "I have brought you here to face your accusers."

The Lady of the Lake stepped forward and the shadows began to separate from her clothing.

"You killed us," the boys' voices startled Richard, who watched the darkness, a curious expression on his face. *"You hung us and sent us to die, alone and afraid."*

Prince John stepped backward as the shadows surged toward him. "Wha—what kind of trickery is this?"

"No trickery," Nyneve said. "You have heard them before." She held out her hands, and more darkness flowed from them to pool on the ground in front of her. While everyone stared, the two ghosts Marian had met on the battlements; Alair and Dalen formed, no longer transparent, but completely solid. Like living boys would be, dressed in their nightclothes. They stared at the prince, faces expressionless, while the shadows oozed across the floor.

The prince's eyes widened until Marian was sure they would roll out of his head and onto the floor. "I—no. Do not allow them to touch me."

Laughter erupted from Dalen and Alair's broken throats. It spiraled up the ceiling and vibrated off the tapestry covered walls.

Marian shrank back against Robin, her hand finding his and holding it tight.

Richard stared silently at his brother while the shadows raged all around him. The guards shifted nervously from foot to foot, but maintained their circle around the prince.

"Enough." He raised one hand and the two boys stopped. "They want answers, John, as do I. Why did you kill them?"

"I did no such—" the prince said. "It was the sheriff."

Nyneve snorted scornfully. "It is easy enough to blame a man who is already dead and buried."

Prince John's eyes widened. "Who killed him, and why?"

"That should not be your primary concern," Richard said. "You should be more concerned with the dozens of spirits here and now."

"W—we were hostages," Dalen floated forward. Brown hair curled over his forehead and the beginnings of a mustache danced across his upper lip.

"Yes," the shadows agreed. *"We remember that."*

"Our fathers sent us here. The prince demanded it." Alair spoke, his voice harsh.

Richard looked around the throne room, at the shadows clinging to nearly every available surface. "...every one of these shadows is a ghost?"

Nyneve nodded.

The king glared at his brother, who shrank back. "You took *all* the Welsh lords sons? John, why would you do such a thing?"

The prince straightened. "You never took hostages, Richard? Never killed them when forced to?"

Richard clenched his hands into fists. "I never killed *children. You* effectively wiped out the entire royal Welsh line, expect for that of the throne. What were you trying to accomplish?"

"I thought to expand our lands!" John roared. "I thought you would appreciate my ingenuity, not punish me for it!"

"We were innocent," Dalen said. *"Asleep in our beds when the guards came."*

"We want the justice you promised us," the shadows whined.

Richard nodded. "And you shall have it." He turned to this brother. "For your loyal service to the crown in my absence, I hereby grant you the well earned title of Earl of Nottingham, with all the privileges and rights contained therein."

Prince John's face flushed and he opened his mouth. Richard held up one hand. "Do not thank me yet, brother." His mouth twisted. "Your duties to your new province demand that you remain within Nottingham Castle for a time period of no less than eight months per year and you must spend two of the remaining four months in London, with me. If I am not in London, then you may do as you wish until it is time to return here."

"But—but the ghosts," the prince protested.

"The ghosts will be glad to keep you company, John. After all, you are the reason for their existence. But—" the king held up one cautionary finger. "None of you are permitted to actually *murder* my brother. He is indolent as well as insolent, but he is still of the Plantagenet line."

"Those terms are acceptable," the shadows replied.

Dalen winked at Prince John before slowly fading out. Alair waved in Marian's direction before following suit. The shadows sank into the marble flooring until the entire room was free of darkness.

"Richard, you cannot mean to do this," Prince John said frantically. "I have been nothing but loyal to you..."

The king laughed bitterly. "Loyal? You plotted to over throw me, allowed your *friend* to imprison not one but *two* women, and could not be bothered to raise enough gold within a year to ransom me from King Leopold's dungeons! That is not loyalty, dear brother. That is incompetence at best, treason at worst."

"I do not believe you." The prince stood a bit taller. "My friend would never have imprisoned anyone."

"Lady Marian, please enlighten my brother on his misconceptions." Richard commanded.

Marian released Robin's hand and stepped closer to the throne.

"The sheriff held Dulcina Scarlett in his dungeons for five years," Marian began. "I learned of her presence unexpectedly." She continued with the story of her kidnapping. The prince's shoulders drooped further with each sentence.

"I did not know," he finally said. "Richard, you cannot believe I would condone such actions!"

"You should have known, John. That was the point." Richard said sadly. "But it does not matter. You shall live by what I have decreed." His face was sober. "The only reason I am not having you killed is because you are my brother. Do not forget my generosity."

It was a clear dismissal. Prince John bowed his head and, under the escort of the four guards, stalked out of the room.

Nyneve smiled. "Well done, Richard. Your father would have been proud."

"Robin, I wish you to see you back within the week, at which time you will receive a formal pardon for your actions." King Richard said. "I will extend the same courtesy to your band of, what do the villagers call them? 'Merry Men'? You all have our eternal gratitude." He smiled. "On a personal note, I wish to be invited to your nuptials, whenever they take place."

Marian blushed while Mother and Father chuckled.

"Stop it, Richard, you are embarrassing the child," Nyneve admonished. She peered at him. "You look tired. Have you slept at all?"

Richard bit out a bitter laugh. "When was I supposed to sleep? Before I dealt with John and the possible demise of my kingdom, or maybe before the ghosts that my brother murdered demanded retribution?"

Nyneve stiffened. "You need rest," she said. "And do not take out your temper on *me*, Richard Plantagenet. Remember, I knew you when you were in the cradle!"

Richard sighed and his huge shoulders sagged. "Leave me," he ordered. "It has been a trying day."

The five of them watched in silence as the king climbed the steps to his throne and slumped down into the seat.

"Come, children," Nyneve herded them out of the room and pulled the door shut. "I need to return to the forest. You may come along if you wish."

"I believe Bea and I shall stay here," Father said. "It has been a long day for all of us, and I think Robin and Marian could use some time to themselves."

Mother nodded her agreement, much to Marian's shock. "Your father and I will begin packing. If I know Richard, he will want us to stay, but I am ready to return home. Court tires me." She winked at Marian, who bit back a giggle. "I know you have missed the forest, Mari. Go and enjoy yourself."

Chapter Thirty-Nine:

Robin and Marian strolled along behind Nyneve. It was only when Robin veered off the main path that Marian realized they were not going back to the heart.

"Where are you taking me?"

Robin smiled. "I thought we could celebrate our betrothal where we first met," he glanced at her. "And, even though it is completely inappropriate, I have the overwhelming desire to kiss you."

Marian's heart fluttered wildly. "Why let inappropriateness stop you?"

He laughed and held a branch out of her way. "Oh, Marian du Luc, I do love you."

She gulped, suddenly nervous. "I—think I love you, as well."

Robin smiled at her. "Was that so difficult to say?"

"Y—yes, I mean, no! No, of course not!" She flushed. "I sound like a fool."

"You sound wonderful," he corrected. "Follow me, it is through here." He stepped through a tangle of green ferns and brown grasses and she followed.

The pool was directly in front of her, only a few feet separated her from the water. "Here?" She smiled. "Why not the in the clearing where we dueled?"

"No, it had to be here," Robin bent low, picking something up and twisting it in his fingers.

"I wish I had something to give you, Marian, but until Richard pardons me all I have is my heart." He knelt in front of her on one bent knee. "And this." He held out his hand, palm up.

She looked down. There, nestled against his tanned skin, lay a small ring of braided grasses.

"Will you allow me to place it on your finger?" Robin asked.

Tears of happiness filled her eyes. She held her left hand out. It trembled.

Robin slipped the ring on, pressing a kiss to the back of her hand. When she sank to the ground, her gown bunched up under her knees. He met her lips with his own.

The kiss was softer than Marian expected. She could hear birds chirping in the oak trees and the small rustle of squirrels in the undergrowth as her eyes slid shut and her lips parted. Her heart began to pound as she leaned toward him, but he pulled away.

"I—cannot, Marian." Robin sounded breathless. "It would not be prudent for us to continue."

"I know," she blushed at what he did not say.

He rose, helping her back to her feet. "We should find Nyneve."

Marian touched her lips as she followed Robin back through the tremendously tall oaks and onto the main path. They felt slightly tender to her fingertips and only made her want to kiss Robin more deeply. She reddened, thankful he could not see her face.

"You are very quiet," Robin turned around, facing her while continuing to walk backward. Dry leaves crunched under his feet.

"I was thinking about Dalen, Alair and the rest of the boys," Marian said quickly. "Do you think they will be able to find peace now?"

Robin smiled, as though he knew she was lying. "The Lady seems to believe it and the ghosts appeared to be happy with Prince John's punishment." He stopped in the middle of the path. "Marian, could you be happy living here?"

"You mean in the forest?"

"It may take a while before I can provide you with a roof over your head." Robin took her hand.

"But…your father was a lord." Marian frowned. "That title is now yours, is it not?"

"True," Robin agreed. "And the king will probably want me at court until my father's duties are settled, but I will ask him for a special dispensation to live here, instead. Court does not suit me."

"You would live here, with me?"

Robin laughed softly. "Yes, Marian. Here, in the forest, with you."

"I would like that very much," Marian admitted. She glanced around, puzzled. "I do not remember this path ending..."

"It normally does not," Nyneve brushed ferns the same color as her gown out of the way as she stepped through them and onto the path. "I moved the heart here temporarily."

"You *moved* part of the forest?!" Marian's eyes were wide.

"Yes," the Lady said. "I felt that would be easiest, since Dulcina is really not well enough to travel long distances."

"She does it more often than she is admitting to," Robin said. "She has used it to help us confound the sheriff and his men on more than one occasion."

"Leave it alone, Robin. She will learn more of my secrets soon enough. In the meantime, come in and be welcomed to my home." Long, bell-like sleeves brushed the ground as Nyneve gestured. "We have been waiting for you."

Marian smiled as she stepped through the massive ferns. Pink blossoms littered the ground below massive dogwood trees. Marian's eyes narrowed when she saw them.

"So *this* is where you got the dogwood," she whispered. "But what I do not understand is how you got from here to the inn so quickly."

Robin smiled. "The Lady honored me with one of her favors."

"The idea of being related to someone so powerful frightens me." Marian shivered.

"She is not so bad," Robin said. "Look, she brought someone to see you."

Marian looked where Robin pointed. Dulcina sat on a moss covered tree stump while Will sat, curled, at her feet.

"Will!" Marian cried happily. She pulled away from Robin and dashed across the clearing. "How long have you been here?!"

Will rose and braced himself as Marian hurled herself at him. "Oof! I have been here long enough to reunite with my mother," he smiled at Dulcina, whose brown eyes looked clear.

"Did Nyneve heal her?" Marian asked.

"Not completely," Nyneve said. "But she is better than she was. It will take time for her mind to heal completely, but she should make a full recovery."

"They have been amazing," Will said. "The Lady Nyneve told me what happened when I arrived." He smiled. "I am so glad you are safe, Marian."

"You risked a great deal to rescue me," Dulcina murmured. The fingers of one hand traced the brand on the other, over and over; like a talisman.

"I could not have left you there," Marian said, stepping away from Will. "But where is Lord Aelfred?"

"He had to return to the castle," Nyneve said. "But he will visit, from time to time. I suspect he is quite fond of Dulcina."

The other woman giggled.

"Speaking of fondness," Nyneve said, "can I see your left hand please, Marian?"

It was an odd request, but Marian held out her left hand. Nyneve took it in hers. "It is a pretty piece of braiding." She brought Marian's hand up to her lips and blew on it.

Marian inhaled sharply; sure her hand was being doused in lightening. Yanking it away, she stared down in amazement. A green and black swirled braided stone ring encircled her finger where the grass ring once rested.

"I think malachite is a much more appropriate choice for a wedding band." Nyneve smiled.

"I—thank you," Marian said. "But we do not know when we will marry, since we have nowhere to live."

"A ceremony is easy enough to perform," the old woman shrugged. "When you are ready, you will know." She turned to Robin, who had stepped back a pace. "As far as where you will live, do you think you and your bride would be happy here?"

"I was hoping that would be an option," Robin admitted. He pulled Marian into his arms and rested his cheek on the top of her head.

"Then it is settled," Nyneve said. She raised her voice slightly. "En'ja, please join us."

The ferns surrounding the clearing parted and a petite woman, nearly half of Marian's modest height, entered the glade. She wore a long gown identical to the one Nyneve had on. It shimmered as she stepped daintily toward Marian.

Tiny iridescent wings flowed out from the woman's back and her delicate face was wreathed in a welcoming smile. Marian gasped in delight.

The fairy's voice was like musical bells, clear and bright. "Welcome to Sherwood."

ℐ ℐ ℐ ℐ

About the Author:

Shanti Krishnamurty lives in Atlanta, Georgia with her husband, two sons and dogs of the gigantic variety.

When she's not busy playing MMORPGs, she attends college online; home educates her children and writes constantly.

She is normally found online via Facebook:
www.facebook.com/shanti.krishnamurty
posting about writing or life in general.

She can also be emailed at:
shantibug@charter.net

23169818R10111

Made in the USA
Charleston, SC
12 October 2013